P9-EDI-693

Emmett

BY L. C. ROSEN

Jack of Hearts (and other parts)

Camp

Lion's Legacy

AS LEV AC ROSEN

All Men of Genius

Woundabout

The Memory Wall

Depth

Lavender House

The Bell in the Fog

Rosen, Lev AC, author.
Emmett

2023
33305255582607
ca   11/03/23

Emmett

L. C. ROSEN

LITTLE, BROWN AND COMPANY
New York   Boston

This book is a work of fiction. Names, characters, places, and incidents are the product of the author's imagination or are used fictitiously. Any resemblance to actual events, locales, or persons, living or dead, is coincidental.

Copyright © 2023 by Lev Rosen

Cover art copyright © 2023 by Allison Reimold. Cover design by Patrick Hulse. Cover copyright © 2023 by Hachette Book Group, Inc. Interior design by Carla Weise.

Hachette Book Group supports the right to free expression and the value of copyright. The purpose of copyright is to encourage writers and artists to produce the creative works that enrich our culture.

The scanning, uploading, and distribution of this book without permission is a theft of the author's intellectual property. If you would like permission to use material from the book (other than for review purposes), please contact permissions@hbgusa.com. Thank you for your support of the author's rights.

Little, Brown and Company
Hachette Book Group
1290 Avenue of the Americas, New York, NY 10104
Visit us at LBYR.com

First Edition: November 2023

Little, Brown and Company is a division of Hachette Book Group, Inc. The Little, Brown name and logo are trademarks of Hachette Book Group, Inc.

The publisher is not responsible for websites (or their content) that are not owned by the publisher.

Little, Brown and Company books may be purchased in bulk for business, educational, or promotional use. For information, please contact your local bookseller or the Hachette Book Group Special Markets Department at special.markets@hbgusa.com.

Library of Congress Cataloging-in-Publication Data
Names: Rosen, Lev AC, author. | Austen, Jane, 1775–1817. Emma.
Title: Emmett / L. C. Rosen.
Description: First edition. | New York : Little, Brown and Company, 2023. | Audience: Ages 14 and up. | Summary: Seventeen-year-old self-absorbed Emmett navigates love and relationships in this queer retelling of *Emma*.
Identifiers: LCCN 2022056411 | ISBN 9780316524773 (hardcover) | ISBN 9780316525183 (ebook)
Subjects: CYAC: Gay men—Fiction. | Interpersonal relations—Fiction. | Love—Fiction. | Grief—Fiction. | High schools—Fiction. | Schools—Fiction. | LCGFT: Romance fiction. | Novels.
Classification: LCC PZ7.1.R67 Em 2023 | DDC [Fic]—dc23
LC record available at https://lccn.loc.gov/2022056411

ISBNs: 978-0-316-52477-3 (hardcover), 978-0-316-52518-3 (ebook)

Printed in the United States of America

LSC-C

Printing 1, 2023

FOR LESLIE

who dealt with a condescending know-it-all

in high school, college, living together,

and even now,

as he dedicates a book to you

chapter one

I KNOW I'M BLESSED. I'M NOT RELIGIOUS AT ALL, BUT THAT'S THE best word for it. I'm good-looking by conventional standards, smart, and my dad has a lot of money. I don't mean all that to sound awful, I'm just stating the facts. I'm very lucky to have been born with all this. The least I can do is try to give back.

So I do that, and do it well: I help out at the food bank on Wednesdays after school, I tutor for free, and I try to make sure I'm a nice person. Which, when combined with everything I've already stated, makes me pretty popular. But that's a good thing, because when you're popular, you have more opportunities to be nice. Like by telling people not to be mean to someone, or setting an example. Or even something small, such as letting people sit with you at lunch, like I've been doing with

Georgia, even though, let's be honest, she's kind of *a lot*. But her best friend, John Feng, is doing the exchange student thing this semester, studying in France, and I guess she just gravitated to me as the most well-known gay guy, since she and John are copresidents of the Queer Alliance. So I let her sit with us at lunch, and talk and talk like she usually does, and I smile, because I'm blessed, and blessed people have to give back.

"John is having the best time in Paris," she says, sighing. She emails with him almost every day and gives us a full report, as though any of us are really friends with John, which we aren't. I know Georgia wants John and me to be a couple. We're both out, happy, handsome, and we vie for top spot in our class rankings, along with Miles. But we're not really great friends. I don't mind him—he's polite, maybe a little withdrawn, a talented pianist—but we're just not close. And besides, I don't do relationships.

"Has he gone to Notre-Dame yet?" asks Miles. "Did he send photos? I want to see how the restoration is coming." Miles is into ruins, old buildings, stuff like that. It's a weird thing to be into, I know. He printed out photos of all the old castles he saw when he went to Scotland, and postered them all over a wall in his room. He says it's a reminder that nothing lasts, which is cynical, but when he says it out loud, he means it happier than that. Almost romantically. He loves a memento mori, he says because they remind him to enjoy the moment.

"Not yet, but look, he went to the Eiffel Tower!" she says, showing him the photo on her phone. "Look!"

But Miles isn't really a romantic. He's like me, never seriously dated, except he's straight. I like to think he's not dating because of me, for the same reasons as me. The ones I convinced him were right. When I was young, my mother, a doctor, told me that your brain keeps growing, and I remember looking it up after she died, when I was fourteen, and discovering she meant it literally: the prefrontal cortex doesn't mature until you're twenty-five. Since then, I've felt a relationship before your brain is developed is silly. You're not in full possession of your impulses or understanding, so you can't promise yourself to someone else. Why get involved with something that's just going to end? Relationships ending are painful. Spare yourself. Simply don't date until your brain might be able to establish something that won't end.

And since Miles and I were closer back when I figured all this out, the way across-the-street-neighbor-kids-whose-moms-were-sorority-sisters are close, I told him that as soon as I decided it. And I think he realized I was right. That's something else I do that's nice—I educate people on why I do things. Even if Miles doesn't appreciate it like he used to. But I'm sure that's why he doesn't date. He's good-looking enough that he could date any girl he wanted. He's gone on a date here and there, but it's never turned into anything. I suppose he might be asexual, but with two moms and a very accepting school environment, I think he would have told someone by now. So I'm sure it's just that he's had the good sense to follow my lead and wait until twenty-five.

"And here he is walking along the River Seine!" Georgia says to Miles, showing us photo after photo of the river, which is definitely beautiful, even if John's photos have diminishing returns on the "breathtaking" thing.

"Breathtaking," I say, hoping it will make her put the phone away. Instead, she turns to her side of the table, where Taylor and West are sitting, gazing into each other's eyes, holding hands and whispering into each other's ears. They giggle sometimes. It's cute. Just because I don't think a relationship before twenty-five is fair to either you or the other person, doesn't mean I'm horrified by other people having them. Taylor is, after all, my best friend. She's wanted a boyfriend since before she told us she was a girl. And I pretty much set her up with West, so I'm happy they're so happy. Even if it means she's been a bit absentee in the friend department. I think that's why Miles has been sitting with us lately. He hasn't really done that in a while, he usually sits with his friends from the debate team, but since Taylor and West hooked up, Miles has been here most days. I think to keep me company because he feels sorry for me, which is sweet, but also a little condescending. A very Miles combination.

I sip my protein smoothie and let my eyes drift away

as Georgia goes on about John in Paris: John at the Louvre, John at the Eiffel Tower, John eating a baguette. The lunchroom is packed, but it's been done up in very soothing off-whites, with low electric light, and large French doors, which are open to the quad, where more tables are set up for those who want to eat outside—I prefer not to, the breeze from the ocean sometimes knocks over water bottles. The chairs all have cushions, and the tables have tablecloths—checked in the school colors: canary yellow and robin's egg blue. Outside, by the doors, is a string quartet that the school brings in to play throughout the day when classes aren't in progress. Music, they say, calms the spirit and encourages learning. I like it when they do covers of pop songs best, but right now they're playing Einaudi's "Fairytale," which feels appropriate.

It all looks more like a country club than a high school, but that's the point of Highbury Academy: for everything to be, as the brochures say, "comfortable and agreeable, so the students can focus on learning and improvement." Even our uniforms are made of breathable cotton jersey, so we may look fancy, but we're not uncomfortable. Taylor says all the yellow and blue makes us look like we should be working in a candy shop, and she's not wrong. We're lucky we have the confidence to pull off the colors.

"You know," Taylor says, interrupting Georgia, "West's brother, Andre, is coming home for the holiday break soon." She says this looking very deliberately at me. I take a bite of my peach and don't make eye contact.

"So what?" Miles asks. "Don't all college kids come home for the holiday break?"

"Well, you know, his family moved here at the end of the summer, and then he went right back to college, so he doesn't know anyone around here. I just think it would be nice if all of us could hang out, so he could make some friends," Taylor says, still staring at me. Taylor's disappearing into coupled bliss is a minor irritant, but her desire to set me up with West's brother is somewhat more abrasive. She knows my opinion on relationships. Although she has shown me his photo and in fairness, he's very attractive, in a film major sort of way, with the half smile and the dark eyes. I take another bite of my peach.

"I'm sure we'll all hang out at some point," I say.

Taylor claps her hands. "I'll throw a party."

Miles raises an eyebrow. "A party for your boyfriend's brother?" His tone is skeptical.

"Oh, it'll be fun," I say so Taylor doesn't have to defend herself, though she just looks amused at the question. "She just wants us all to be friends." I don't tell him he's being condescending. That would be unkind.

"I'll tell John!" Georgia says, already sending the email on her phone.

"Hey, Emmett." I look up at Harrison, who's walking over to us. His tie is a little loose. His tie is always a little loose, but it suits him well enough. "Think you could come over after school and tutor me in chem a little? I need some help."

I nod and take out my phone, checking my calendar. I add *tutor Harrison* after school. "Sure thing," I say. "Do you need a lift after school?"

"Nah," he says. "I have the car today."

"Then I'll see you there," I say.

Harrison nods and smiles, walking away.

"You tutor juniors?" Georgia asks, still typing into her phone. "You are so nice."

"You are so good at that," Harrison says, panting, as he falls back on his damp sheets.

I grin. "Thank you," I say, staring at his ceiling, letting all the postcoital hormones run through me, easing tension, creating happiness. I may think romance before twenty-five is pointless, but the hormonal teenage body has needs, and Harrison is good at fulfilling them. He's attractive, enthusiastic, and very good with his tongue. He leans over me and starts kissing down the front of my chest and I can feel my body start to respond again already. Above us, his ceiling fan whirs softly. I glance at my phone on the nightstand, wondering if we have time for another round.

He stops kissing and I can feel his eyes on me so I bend my neck to look at him hovering over my navel.

"You ever want a boyfriend?" he asks. Immediately, all the good effects of the postcoital hormones flee my body. I can feel my heart rate quicken, my body tense. All the excellent results of the effort of the past hour and a half evaporate in a flash.

"No," I say, sitting up and looking around the room for my shirt.

"Relax," he says, pushing me back onto the bed. "I know we're no strings. I'm just asking."

He rests his head on my chest and I take a deep breath. At this point he owes me another round just to cancel out what he's done. I run my hand down his shoulder, down his spine.

"I guess I just mean I think *I* want one," he says, squeezing his arm around my waist.

I stop moving my hand. I like Harrison, but I absolutely don't want him as a boyfriend.

"You do?" I ask. The more I turn the idea in my head, the more surprising it is. Harrison seemed a safe choice in the no-romance way. He was the one who propositioned me last year, after all. And he's hot: broad and a little soft, with a nice ass and dark curls that fall over his green eyes and pearly skin. He asked me one day after an English class if I'd like to spend some time with him. That was how he phrased it, which I liked. I told him I didn't date, and he said he knew that. He was new last year, but we knew each other in passing—there are several out guys in school, and we're not all friends, but we all know each other on sight, say hi to each other in the halls. But I said yes to spending time with him, and since then, we've established a quick code: tutoring. With my other two gentlemen, we usually just texted. But they both graduated last year, so now it was just Harrison. And he, apparently, is looking for a boyfriend. I frown at the fan. It spins away, amused by my situation.

"I mean, yeah," Harrison says. "I think it would be nice, to hold hands in the hallway, go to prom with someone."

"I guess," I say, shrugging. I've never really thought much of it.

He laughs. "I know, I know, not for you. But just FYI, if I find a boyfriend, then our tutoring days are probably over."

"Of course," I say, wondering who's left to replace him.

"I think Robert might ask me out. You know him?"

I pause, trying to conjure up a face for the name.

"He's on student council with you, president of the environmental club?"

"Yes, yes, of course," I say. "I didn't think he was your type."

"What?" Harrison asks, turning to narrow his eyes at me. "What's my type?"

"Well," I say, looking down the stretch of my body.

"Oh." Harrison laughs. "Yeah, tall, blond, with broad

shoulders and a jawline you could cut someone with? That's everyone's type."

I laugh, blushing a little. "You didn't mention my six-pack," I say, tapping my stomach.

He leans down and kisses just above my navel again. I sigh softly, but he lies back on the bed and puts his arms under his head. "I mean, I don't think I really have a type," he says.

I think of him in the bed with Robert, instead of me. Robert is nice. Sort of thin, and his hair never seems to do what it's supposed to, but he's passionate about whales, I think, which is nice. Or maybe it's rain forests? Super important, whichever one, of course. There's no doubt he's a nice person.

But I like sleeping with Harrison. He's a sexual partner of quality, and that means if he *must* have a boyfriend, then that boyfriend should be of quality, too. And being a good person isn't enough; there need to be shared interests, that spark of special-ness. I saw it between Taylor and West. I just can't imagine it with Harrison and Robert.

"You could do better than Robert, I think," I say, pulling on my briefs.

"Better than?"

"Sorry, that came out rude. I just mean you shouldn't say yes to Robert just because you want a boyfriend. If he asks you out."

"But I do want a boyfriend," he says, turning onto his side to look at me.

"Do you want it to be him specifically, though?" I ask.

"I mean...maybe?"

"Maybe isn't very convincing," I say, smiling at him, an idea suddenly bubbling in my brain.

"But I *do* want a boyfriend," he says. "And Robert is—"

"Then I'll find you one."

He laughs. "What? *You* will?"

"What?" I say, kneeling on the bed next to him. "I set up Taylor and West, you know. And I know how... extraordinary you are, physically," I add, stroking his chin. "I won't have you settle. I'll find someone deserving of you." I reach down and pull on my socks. They're blue, covered in little stethoscopes. Our socks are the one thing we can go crazy with without violating uniform rules.

"Who would you find for me, then?" he asks as I stand and pull my pants on. "Or is this just some complicated scheme to keep me single for our hookups?"

"I assure you, it's not," I say. I smile at him, but he looks a little offended. "I enjoy our rendezvous, of course, but I don't want to stand in the way of you being happy. We're friends. I want you to be happy."

"We're friends?" He smiles.

"Aren't we? You eat lunch with me sometimes. We talk, we spend time at each other's houses."

"That last one doesn't count," he says, laughing. "But sure, okay, we're friends."

"Then let me do what I do for my friends and find you a perfect match."

"Who else have you done it for, besides Taylor?" he asks, raising an eyebrow.

"Well," I say, looking back up at the fan for a moment, "no one. Yet. But you'll be next. I like it. I like making people happy."

"Oh?" He pushes himself back up, his muscled shoulders supporting his torso as he brings his face close to mine. One dark curl falls over his eyes. "Well, until you make me happy that way, there are other ways you can make me happy."

I glance at my phone again, then take my socks back off. I still have a little time before I need to be home.

"Emmett?" Dad calls the moment I come through the door. "Is that you? Where have you been?"

I sigh and close the door behind me. "Tutoring," I call back. "I texted you."

We have a lovely home. Dad's a money manager who works from home and comes from wealth, and Mom was a surgeon, which is how we can afford to live in a very nice house in Highbury, one of the richest districts of California, just north of LA. Dad thinks it's important that we're here—there's fairly low air pollution for California and the weather is usually sunny. The house is a sort of Frank Lloyd Wright–inspired ranch, with a pool and flower garden out back and lots of glass walls so the light comes through. Dad likes that. Sunlight is healthy, and Dad is always worried about healthy.

"I know, I know you texted," Dad says, coming down the stairs. He's holding a syringe. One of those days, then. Yes, it's a lot. Dad can sometimes be a lot. He went to online nursing school after Mom died just in case I needed some extra medical attention—and he often feels I do. But he never takes blood without my permission. He just asks a lot. For him, it's like asking how I'm doing. But I'm doing just fine today so I smile broadly and walk by him.

"I was just worried," he says. "I should take some of your blood. We can send it in for a test."

"Dad, the doctor did my blood work last month," I say, walking past him. "I'm fine." He's been getting more anxious lately, I think because I'm going to Stanford next year. So I have to be firm with him about this sometimes.

I hear him sigh as I put my backpack down on the dining room table and start fishing out my books. I like doing my homework in the living room. It's where Mom used to help me study. She also decorated the house. The foyer with the big staircase and the huge windows is wallpapered in this giant flower print, with white tile floors, but then you come back here, to the open living/dining/kitchen area, and its wood floors, glass doors out to the porch, and French-blue walls, and it looks out on the garden, which is always filled with flowers. Dad loves flowers, and so did Mom. It's cozy back here. Sometimes I think it still smells like her perfume, too. Like lime and basil.

"You're not having sex, right?" Dad says, coming up behind me. "Sex is so dangerous, Emmett." This is the other main theme of his medical anxieties. Maybe I should have texted earlier instead of waiting until I was leaving Harrison's. Normal parents, from what I understand, worry about their kids being in car crashes if they haven't heard from them. But with Dad, if he wonders where I am, that worry somehow leads to my health, and then he spirals.

"Relax, Dad," I say as calmly as I can. "I know to use condoms." I pause. I hate the lie I'm about to tell. "But not until I'm ready to have sex."

Dad knows I'm gay. He doesn't care about that. It's sex of any kind—gay, straight, bi, pan, orgiastic—that concerns him.

"Yes, yes, good. Be careful. Boys can catch HPV, too." He squeezes my shoulder and I take his hand for a moment. Mom died of cervical cancer almost four years ago now.

"I know, Dad," I say. "That's why I got vaccinated. But I promise, I'll be careful."

"Okay," he says. "Poor Taylor, getting all mixed up in dating. So dangerous, and we see so much less of her.

She used to be here every day after school...." He sighs. Dad loves Taylor. She always loves walking through the flower garden with him, and we usually came here after school to hang out and study, which he liked because then he knew where I was.

He sighs and looks at the syringe he's holding. "I'll go put this away." He heads back toward the stairs. "Next month, though. Just in case."

The doorbell rings and I glance up. It's odd for someone to drop by. Dad heads for the door. Actually, no, there's one person who drops by.

"Miles!" Dad says, excited.

"Hi, Henry," Miles says. I can hear them hug. I think Dad likes Miles more than I do. I stand up and go into the foyer. No, I'm certain Dad likes Miles more than I do.

"Hi," I say, smiling as brightly as I can. "What are you doing here?" I don't want to be rude, of course, and Miles does this. He lives right across the street, it's not a long walk, and our families are very close, so he's always welcome, but I do have homework.

"Your dad texted my mom," Miles said. "He wanted to know where you were. I didn't see your car in the driveway, so she sent me over...."

"Dad." I sigh. "I was tutoring." I turn back to Miles. "It's supposed to rain tonight, so I parked in the garage."

"You didn't text me back," Dad says, turning on me. "I was worried. You could have been in a car accident."

I take out my phone. I have a missed text from Dad. He sent it while I was driving.

"I was driving home by then," I say.

"Yes, well, you came home a few minutes later."

"So how long did you wait to text Jasmine after I didn't respond?" I try to keep my voice calm.

"I don't know," Dad says. "A while, though."

"You texted me ten minutes ago," I say, holding up my phone. "The walk from Miles's door to ours is five minutes. You waited five minutes."

"I was worried," Dad says.

"Well, you're home," Miles says, "so I can go—"

"No, no," Dad says. "Stay for dinner. Invite your mother over. We can all eat together."

Miles looks at me, and I smile. Dad invited him to stay, after all. I'm not going to tell him to go just so I can get some work done without his superior sneer hovering over me—that wouldn't be nice.

"I'm just doing some homework," I say. Dad heads upstairs to put away the syringe, finally. I turn and walk back into the dining room. Miles comes and sits down next to me. He's changed out of the school uniform and is in a mint-green V-neck and white skinny jeans. I suddenly feel a little awkward still in my school-issued pale gray slacks, white shirt, and yellow tie with the blue-and-yellow sweater vest over it. I pull the vest off, but it gets stuck partway and I flail for a moment, pulling.

Miles stands and pulls it off for me.

"I didn't need your help," I tell him, folding the vest and putting it on the table.

"You looked like you did," he says, smiling in that condescending way he likes to smile.

"Well, I didn't," I say, and loosen my tie. I know I should say thank you, to be nice, but Miles is just so insufferable with his "I know better" attitude and stepping in when he's not asked to. That's why we went from best friends to...whatever we are now. Friends-ish? Family friends? It was just one too many little notes on how I could do something better, how the nice thing I did wasn't nice enough.

"I was just trying to be *nice*," he says. I look up at him, glaring. He said *nice* with extra honey in it, like he was making fun of me for all the times when I say I want to be nice. I used to tell him that was important to me, when we talked more. Maybe I'm reading too much into it. I turn back to my books.

Nothing is ever good enough for Miles, and this year, when he chose to start sitting with the debate team at lunch instead of with me, he made it clear that I, in particular, had failed to live up to his standards. I'm still not entirely sure what I did. It's not like we had a falling-out. Last year seemed normal, and then over the summer he was volunteering at the hospital and we didn't see each other as much, but on the first day back, though I clearly left a seat for him, he went and sat with the debate team. I didn't make a thing of it, that would be rude, but I admit I was a bit stung. But I've gotten over it. Realized it was a relief, really. It's not like we don't see each other practically every day, being neighbors and all. Maybe he just needed a break from me the way I so often need a break from him these days. Though I am much more pleasant to be around.

"Must have been tutoring for a while," he says, walking around the room, looking at the chairs.

"What?" I ask. "And it's over there." I point to the kitchen, where a fleece throw is. Miles grins and goes over to it and wraps it around his shoulders and comes back to sit down.

He pulls the blanket tight around him. He loves that blanket of ours, with its fleece lining. It's a silly thing we got online, with some flowers I thought would match the color of the walls, but don't, and so look off. But he loves it, so I don't throw it out—it would make him too sad, and that wouldn't be nice.

"You were tutoring Harrison Stein, right?" he asks, once the blanket is sufficiently cozy.

"Yes." I open my AP Bio textbook and flip the pages.

"He gets straight As."

"I'm an excellent tutor," I say, not looking up.

"What subject do you tutor him in?"

"Bio," I say, because the book is in front of me.

"He's taking chem."

"He wants to prepare," I say, glancing up at Miles, a bit surprised he knows Harrison's schedule—I didn't think they were especially close. "Why are you asking? Do you need tutoring?"

"I'm getting straight As in bio already."

"Well, I guess we're all very clever, then."

"Not as clever as some might think," he says, reaching out and tugging on my collar.

I bat his hand away and look down. My shirt is buttoned up wrong; an extra buttonhole lies empty at the collar. My tie was covering it.

"Huh," I say.

"Pretty sure you had those buttoned right before tutoring."

I roll my eyes. "Are you going to let me do my homework, or are you just going to pester me with random sartorial commentary?"

He laughs. "You're something else, Emmett. But yeah, let me text my mom and invite her over."

I flip through the pages and try to focus on the work, but I can feel my face scowling. Damn know-it-all Miles. Why would he even mention it? Why rub it in my face that he's made an assumption about me and it happens to be right—a lucky guess really. What does it give him, aside from some perverse satisfaction?

No. I will not dwell on this. Miles isn't a gossip, so he won't spread his theories—however correct they may be—around school. Which is good, because I don't need that. The gossiping, people assuming that just because I have sex with a friend sometimes we must also be romantically involved. The fetishizing. The "You guys are so adorable" from girls I've barely spoken to, as though saying that is somehow allyship. Even Georgia, queer and cohead of the Queer Alliance, will jump on that boat, telling us we're so cute, asking us to pose for photos, going on about the "inspiring joy of visible queer love." She does it with the other queer boys in school when they couple up.

I'm still dwelling, I realize. Obsessing maybe. I turn back to my pages for the ninetieth time.

"Okay," Miles says, putting down his phone. "Mom will be over in a sec."

"Great," I say, not looking up.

"Did you not want us to stay?"

"No," I say, and it sounds fake. "No," I repeat, getting it right this time. "I'm just worried about all the work I have."

"You can do it after dinner," Dad says, coming into the room. He's put on a faded purple polo shirt and jeans. "Now we're ordering pizza and having dinner with our dearest friends."

He smiles at us and Miles smiles back and I smile, too, because otherwise I'm the mean one.

"Wait," I say, realizing what he just said. "Pizza? From that new place? Dad, no."

"It's so healthy," Dad says to Miles. "Cauliflower crusts!"

"They put tea in the tomato sauce."

"Green tea," Dad says. "It fights free radicals. And they have this one pie topped with blueberries!"

"Dad, I told you last time, I didn't enjoy it. I will have a glass of iced green tea if it will make you feel better. But we're ordering real pizza. From the organic place."

Dad sighs.

I stand and go to the fridge and take out a pitcher of iced green tea, which I make every morning, and pour myself a glass. "Healthy," I say, then sip from it. "See?"

Dad frowns. "The pizza wasn't so awful."

"I'll try it," Miles says.

I shoot him a death glare, then make myself stop. "That's very kind of you to say, but there are times when politeness must be discarded in favor of self-preservation."

"That bad?" Miles asks.

I nod.

"Hello?" calls Jasmine, Miles's mom, from the foyer.

"We're back here, Jas," Dad calls out.

Jasmine rounds the corner, a big smile on her face. She's blond with full high cheeks that look like Miles's, though Miles has the coloring of his other mom, Priyanka. Jasmine carried him, but I'm not sure which egg was used, or where the sperm came from, but somehow he manages to look like both of them. Priyanka's bronze skin and dark gold eyes, Jasmine's face shape and bright smile.

I love Jasmine. It was Priyanka who was Mom's best

friend, the two of them having gone to college and med school together. They were always across the street, always coming over, but then Mom died, and Priyanka and Jasmine, I think, tried to make sure they were in my life to check that I was okay, and Dad too. So they never stopped coming over. Last year, Priyanka decided to do Doctors Without Borders and has been away helping out in South Africa since, so I think Jasmine likes the company, too.

"Please tell my father we can't order from the pizza place that puts green tea in the sauce," I tell her.

She grins, holding back a laugh. "It's an interesting idea, but they go too far, and the tea is overbrewed, makes it bitter," she says. "If I wanted to do that, I'd use white tea, and I'd just put it in the crust, with some citrus, too."

"You're not cooking," I tell her, then look over at Dad. "I won't have you invited over just to work."

"I didn't ask her to," Dad says.

Jasmine has a cooking show, and like half a dozen bestselling cookbooks. And we love her food. But inviting someone over and then having them cook is the height of rudeness.

"Let's just order regular pizza," I say.

"That sounds great," Jasmine says, putting her arm around Miles's shoulder.

"Well, all right," Dad says, looking meaningfully at the glass of iced tea I'm holding.

I take a long gulp. It's cool and pleasantly grassy. Dad

takes out his tablet and after picking out toppings and ordering, we sit down on the porch while we drink iced tea and wait for the pizza to show up.

Dad has a rocking chair out here, and he sits in it, facing Miles, Jasmine, and me on the large swing. We look out over the pool and the flower garden that Dad works on year-round. The sun is setting, turning the sky a beautiful pink.

"The jasmine is blooming, as it always does in your honor," Dad says to Jasmine.

She laughs. "You always say that."

"It's always true!" Dad says, very serious. "And the roses always bloom for Pri. They've been looking so sad. When does she come home?"

"Soon," Jasmine says, smiling. "A few weeks."

"Right after midterms," Miles says.

"In time for the winter carnival!" I say. "You can bring her."

"Yeah," Miles says. "That'll be fun. You and Ma can stop by after my shift at the ticket booth." Miles and I are both part of the student council committee for the winter carnival, along with Taylor, and Harrison, and a bunch of other people. We throw the carnival at school and proceeds are split between a school improvement project and a charity of the council's choosing. Technically, I'm president of the committee, but I'm not a control freak about it or anything. We're all doing it together, that's what I tell everyone.

"It's going to be excellent this year," I say. "Fair But Frozen Maid, that new ice cream shop in LA with the trucks, is sending one to be there all day. They have the most exquisite flavors. One is green tea blueberry," I add, turning to Dad. "And of course rides and games."

"Emmett made it his quest to get the Fair But Frozen Maid truck," Miles says.

"It was a team effort," I say. "But I do think it'll be a big draw."

"I love the winter carnival," Dad says. "Freshman year, you remember, Miles won you that rabbit toy?"

I roll my eyes. "Yeah, Dad." That was when we were best friends.

"Is that ride coming back?" he asks. "With the penguins?"

We all laugh. "Yes," I say. "The little bouncing penguin ride for six-year-olds will be there."

"There's no age limit on it!" Dad says, laughing. "I love that ride."

"We know," Jasmine says, laughing.

"The penguins are very cute," Dad adds, making us all laugh again.

"Well, I promise it will be there," I say. "I triple-confirmed it with the rental place. Also the long drop, the teacups...I should write back to the fried dough place, though, they haven't confirmed check-in time."

"You're so busy," Jasmine says to me. "Both of you.

I don't think I was this busy when I was your age, with tests and fundraisers and triple-confirming with vendors."

"And tutoring," Miles says with a smirk. "Emmett tutors, too."

"I like to give back," I say, keeping my face calm. "I actually decided that, fresh off the success of setting up my friend Taylor with her new boyfriend, I'm going to try to set up my friend Harrison, too."

"Harrison?" Miles says. The smirk is gone. "Is that a good idea?"

"Why not?" I say. "He wants a boyfriend, I want to find him one. I'm good at it. A natural intuition."

"Just because you set up Taylor and West doesn't mean you have a natural intuition," Miles says, his voice going up a bit, "and considering you...tutor him, don't you think that's sort of a conflict of interest?"

"Not at all. I know him very well," I say, smiling.

"Well, I think it's a nice idea," Jasmine says, her Southern accent creeping out like honey leaking from a jar. "Matchmakers can be wonderful, y'know? As long as it's about compatibility and not, like, family esteem or breeding or anything. Just introducing people and seeing if they like each other. I think that's nice."

"And of course being in a monogamous relationship with only one sexual partner significantly reduces your risks of STDs," Dad says.

"Condoms work, Dad," I say. "And nonmonogamous relationships are just as valid as monogamous ones."

"If no one wants the monogamy," Miles says. "But I like monogamy, I'm just a romantic like that." He raises an eyebrow, goading me.

I turn to him, glaring, about to say something less than nice, but thankfully the doorbell rings, interrupting me. "I'll get it and set the table," I say.

"I'll help," Miles says, also standing. He says it like he wants to talk to me.

"What nice kids you are," Jasmine says.

I walk to the door quickly, hoping Miles will just set the table, but he follows me to the door, whispering.

"You're going to set up Harrison with someone? You're sleeping with him, Emmett."

"I don't know what you're talking about. And what's this about you being a romantic? That was a joke, I hope."

"Don't change the subject," he says as I make it to the door and open it. "I've known you long enough to know when you're screwing someone."

The pizza delivery guy looks between us, holding out two boxes.

"Uh, Woodhouse?" he asks.

"Yes, thank you," I say, taking the pizza and giving him a generous tip.

"Even if I were engaging in some mutual pleasure with him," I whisper, "what does that matter?"

"So he's just some guy you tutor and screw?"

"I don't actually tutor him, Miles. He's very bright."

"I know, I mean…it's separate? Really?"

"Sure. We're friends. We do…friendly things together."

"You and I don't do those friendly things," he says, taking the pizzas from me.

"You're straight," I say. "But if you weren't, and we were sleeping together, I don't think it would change much about our friendship."

He turns and walks back into the dining room. "I think it would," he says. "And I think if you were really his friend, you'd want more for him."

"So you weren't kidding, you have gone *romantic* all of a sudden?" I say, unable to keep the disappointment out of my voice. "I've told you, before twenty-five—"

"The brain isn't done developing, you don't know who you are, yeah yeah." He puts the pizzas down and I take out plates and napkins. "But if you're already having sex with him, and you like him, I don't understand why you wouldn't want to be his boyfriend."

"We're friends, it's not…" I put the plates down on the table. "I'm queer. My closest friends, the people who really get me, they're also going to be the people I sleep with, and when I'm ready for it, my dating pool. Sex, friendship, romance, all in one spot. So sometimes the sex is part of friendship instead of part of romance. That's fine. What's important is keeping everything neat. Making sure everyone knows what the relationship is and where they stand. Nothing messy."

"And you don't want a boyfriend at all?"

"One day," I say.

"You're sure you're not aro?" He raises an eyebrow.

"I'm sure. I've had crushes, romantic fantasies…"

"Yeah?" He smiles, all mischief. "On whom?"

I glare. He will not be getting that out of me, he'll just use it to mock me. Everyone has a crush on the boy next door at some point, right? Mine was for a few months freshman year, and thankfully now is very over.

"But then," I continue, ignoring his question, "I think about the inevitable breakups, the tedious dividing of friends, the conflict after. The…anguish," I add, my eyes inadvertently darting toward the porch. "A romantic relationship is a risk, and before twenty-five, it's almost guaranteed failure. I don't need that pain now. I'll do that later, when we're all adults, with fully grown brains, and there's a chance the relationship works and we never break up and I never have to…For now…friendship, sex. It's less messy."

"I don't know about that," Miles says. "Seems like it would be more messy. And you know, it sounds a little sad. Not all breakups are—"

"Thank you so much for your opinion," I say, then turn away and poke my head outside to where Dad and Jasmine are still sitting. "Dinner!"

chapter two

WHEN I PICK TAYLOR UP THE NEXT DAY, I'M STILL FEELING A BIT annoyed with Miles. It's none of his business who I sleep with, or who I set up, or even who I date, if I were to date.

"Uh-oh," she says, hopping into the passenger seat of my EQS, "what happened? You have that 'I need to be a good person but I just want to punch someone' face."

That makes me laugh, and I shake my head as I start driving us to school. "My dad invited Miles and his mom over last night, which is fine, but when I said I was going to find a boyfriend for Harrison, Miles got all judgy, the way he does. Said it was a bad idea."

The best thing about Taylor is I can tell her anything. I can even be mean about other people to her. She understands. I have all these really just bitchy thoughts sometimes, and they're terrible, and I would never say them aloud, but with Taylor, she won't judge. She says we're all allowed to vent.

It was one of the first things she told me when we met freshman year—she said you need someone you can always be honest with about how you're feeling, because sometimes scary truths have to be spoken aloud. I remember we were sitting on the porch swing on my deck, and it felt like she was trying to tell me something, but what I thought of immediately was how much I missed my mom. And how weird it was, being at a new school, not just having to come out again but having to explain that my mom was dead. It felt like a lot. She took my hand, which I thought might have been romantic back then, because I still thought she was a gay guy like me, but then she looked at me, and I knew it wasn't like that. I knew this was a friend who just wanted me to know it was okay to feel...rough.

"That all sounds hard," she said. "But I'll be there with you."

That's when I knew I'd met my closest friend since Miles.

"Why does Miles think you playing matchmaker is a bad idea?" she asks as I drive. "You did so well with me and West!"

"Right?" I say. "It's like he doesn't want other people to be happy. I'm just trying to do good, give back."

"And you totally will. I know you'll find someone great for Harrison."

"Thank you." I nod firmly.

"Oh, you know who I think likes him? Robert. From carnival planning, you know? I think he's president of the environmental club?"

"Yeah...I think I can find someone better. I like Harrison. He shouldn't just settle for the first guy who comes along."

She laughs. "True. But don't hold him up to your standards."

I sneak a sideways glance at her. So maybe I don't tell her *everything*. The thing is, Taylor is very romantic, so I try to keep my no-strings-attached rendezvous from her because I worry that then she'd try even harder to find me a boyfriend. She wouldn't fetishize me the way Georgia would, but she'd just be so insistent that we should go out and experience love. She says my twenty-five rule is absurd and people are going to get their hearts broken one way or another anyway, so who cares. That's part of love. And I agree—it's just not a part I especially want to experience yet.

She catches me looking and holds her hand up to her earrings, steadying them for me to look when we stop at a red light. "Do you like?"

"Love," I say.

Taylor is gorgeous, green eyes, peachy skin, and dark brown hair that she has in a braid today. Over the summer she transitioned from hormone blockers to estrogen, and though she was pretty before that, since then she's just been so much happier, and it shows—she's always glowing. She's got super-cute earrings on today, too. They're little yellow crystals that match her uniform. Technically, we have a whole wardrobe to choose from for our uniform—always a white shirt, but then it's mix and match: ties in yellow, blue, or yellow-and-blue plaid. Pale gray suit (pants or skirt), or gray, yellow-and-blue-plaid suit. Sweater vest or cardigan in the yellow-and-blue plaid. They're keen on making sure we have a uniform look at Highbury, to make sure no one feels like they have to chase brands or trends, but they still want us to be able to express ourselves. Today Taylor is in the plaid suit, with skirt, and the earrings are blue metal hoops with yellow crystals dangling in the center. They match everything perfectly.

"Thanks! I made them."

"Really? Those are amazing, Taylor. Did you buy new supplies?"

"Yeah, I found a new place that sells metal, and I loved this blue stuff."

Taylor wants to be a jewelry designer. Accessories, too. But she started with jewelry because it's one of the things we can wear to school. I have several brooches she made me and I wear one every day. Today's is a cameo of a woman's profile, surrounded by golden flowers, with chains looping down from it. She calls her aesthetic *extravagant romanticism* because she wants everything to feel sort of vintage but in a modern way—cameo pins with huge flowers, rings with huge flowers, pretty much anything with these huge metal flowers she casts from wax. She says she likes molding things and then seeing them shine, because it's like remaking the world, even the boring stuff—wax, metal—into beautiful things that gleam. I love that about her. That she can see even the most boring things, or ugly things, and turn them into something stunning in her mind, and then will actually do it with her hands.

"Well, I love them," I say, smiling at the earrings again.

"I'm trying to broaden my portfolio before I send it in to FIT next week."

"Well, I think those are fantastic. They'll get you in for sure."

"Thanks," she says in a soft voice. I reach out and squeeze her hand. FIT is her dream school. I got into Stanford early decision last week, which means we'll be on opposite sides of the country, and that always makes my body ache a little to think about. Like the potential distance is already pulling us apart and we're still reaching for each other, arms stretching out. That kind of ache. But I also want her to go to her dream school. I want her to have all of her dreams.

"You're going to get in," I say. "I know it."

"Well, I need to send in this application before midterms or I won't focus on studying at all, so I have like six days left to make my best stuff ever."

"And you will."

"Okay, okay." She shakes her head and I take my hand back. "Let's talk about something else, this is making me anxious."

"What else?" I ask.

"How about Andre, West's brother?" she asks, leaning toward me.

"Taylor, I've told you..."

"I know, I know. But it would be so fun if we were dating brothers! And then, if we all got married, we'd be related. And we'd definitely have to keep in touch no matter what coasts we're on."

"We're going to keep in touch no matter what," I promise her.

"I know..." She sighs. "It would be fun, though. And he says you're hot."

"You did not show him a picture of me."

"I didn't," she says. "But West did. Only fair since I showed you his photo, right?"

"He's a college sophomore. I don't see us making a lasting relationship happen."

"He's a sophomore at Stanford."

"Oh," I say. "You never mentioned that."

"Well, every time I mention him you tell me it's not happening. I can't get a word in edgewise."

I smirk at that and pull into the school parking lot. "I'm just not looking for a boyfriend."

"Well, at least be nice to him when you meet him," she says.

I park the car and laugh. "I'm always nice. And I'm happy to meet him. Maybe he'll be a good match for Harrison."

"Oy vey," Taylor says, opening her door. "I hand you a smart, good-looking man and you palm him off to the guy you're tutoring. I do not understand it."

"I know, but you love me anyway," I say, stepping out of the car.

She narrows her eyes at me over the top of the car, but she's smiling. "Yeah, I do."

We head together toward the main building, where West is waiting. Seeing Taylor run up to him and kiss him, I almost, for a moment, envy them. They just seem so happy, the sun hitting them as they kiss on the white steps leading up to the building, his arms around her waist, her foot up in the air. A few stray leaves from the maple trees even rain down on them, the breeze washing them around the lovestruck couple. Cover of a romance novel. In the distance I can hear the faint melody of the school's string quartet practicing.

They break, and as if reading my mind, Taylor turns to me and says, "Sure you don't want a boyfriend?"

"Are you really still bothering him about that?" West asks, then turns to me, shaking his head. "Sorry, man. It wasn't even my idea."

"I know," I say. I like West. He's straightforward, kind, and handsome, with brown skin, an excellently done fade, and beautiful, high cheekbones. And he's tall, very tall, and surprisingly well muscled for how narrow he is. But more than that, he's just calm. He seems unbothered by everything and like someone who never judges, not even in his head, which is practically impossible to imagine. But that's him. Calming. He's good for Taylor.

"Like my new earrings?" Taylor asks him.

"Are those the ones you've been working on? They came out great, babe."

"Yeah?"

"Yeah." He takes her hand and kisses it, staring in her eyes while a few more leaves circle around them in the breeze. Then they head up the steps into the building and I follow them, quickly forgotten as she tells him about the earrings, and which ones she'll make next. That's fine. I have my own project to worry about: a boyfriend for Harrison.

The string quartet seems to pick up on my goal, as their cover of "thank u, next" breezes through the halls and seafoam-green lockers. I look around me, taking

mental note of any of the queer men I know: There's
Jimmy, he's good-looking, and a junior like Harrison, but
he has a boyfriend at some other school. Alex, a sophomore, but he's always going on about his bird, and I like
birds and all, but it's like it's his whole personality. Adam
is always in his sketch pad, I don't think he's looked up
in years. Tom went to Toronto Pride last year and it's literally all he talks about now. Cale is a horror guy, to the
point where if you can't have a two-hour conversation on
Pinhead with him, there's no point even talking to him.
Ethan smokes pot too often for it to be considered "rec-
reational" anymore. There are so many out guys, and yet
none of them seem right.

I stop in front of my locker—right next to Taylor's—
and put some books away.

"Hey, Emmett." I look around and spot Robert coming over to me. The one who likes Harrison already. He's
a sweet kid, and not bad-looking in theory. But a little
hair product would help, and probably a haircut, and
those glasses are too big for his face, and he needs to
shave better, and his arms are just too thin. I try to imagine him doing to Harrison the things I do to Harrison,
and it just doesn't fit. Though I shouldn't think strictly
physically. He gets good grades, I think. He's head of
the environmental club, so that's good. It's just...the
moment he leaves the room, I tend to forget about him.
Harrison deserves better than forgettable.

"Emmett?" Robert asks again, and I realize I've been staring at him in silence.

"Yes?" I ask, closing my locker.

"You said to come by your locker and grab the form from you for the environmental club booth at the winter carnival, remember? We're doing a lottery, with a big plush whale as the prize. It's so cute, you just wanna squish it!" He laughs a little and pushes his glasses up. No, he won't do.

"Sure," I say, opening my locker again and taking out one of the forms. "Just turn it in to the student activities office."

"I know, I'm on the winter carnival student board, remember?"

"Yes, of course, sorry." I shake my head. "Habit. I say it to everyone who I give a form."

He laughs. "Just running on autopilot. Yeah, I do that. I never remember turning on the radio to NPR when I get home. I just go into my room, and hit the stereo, and then I'm taking off my jacket or fishing out my books and it's like 'Wait, who turned the radio on?'"

"Yes, like that," I say.

"Well, I'll see you at the meeting after school. And I'll have the form done by then."

"Great," I say, closing my locker. "See you later!"

I turn around to find Taylor and West leaning against her locker, lips firmly fastened together. I turn back around and head to class.

I spend all day checking out guys—for Harrison, not just for fun. At lunch, though, inspiration strikes, and I know exactly who to set Harrison up with: Clarke. Cocaptain of the cheerleading squad, and so very well-built, with red-blond hair and bright blue eyes. Clarke is popular, and a solid student. He's also a professional gymnast who everyone says could make the Olympic team in a few years. He's a junior, same as Harrison, and has like 47k followers on KamerUhh, that social media site with the videos and photos, which makes him almost famous. I only have 10k, but I'm barely on social media really—I post some selfies sometimes, but mostly I just lurk, watching other people's videos. Clarke is all over KamerUhh, with photos of him stretching, at the gym, in a Speedo at the pool, and doing videos where he lip-syncs, explains various cheer throws, or does whatever the viral trend of the week is. He's super charming, and really funny. Everyone likes Clarke, even when he's a little bitchy.

Harrison will be perfect for him—they'll look great together, and Harrison's sincerity will balance Clarke's sometimes too-camera-ready exterior. Meanwhile Clarke's outgoingness will help bring Harrison out of his shell a bit. He's perfect.

"Clarke," I tell Taylor, who's eating next to me, one

hand spooning yogurt out of its cup, the other entwined with West's hand on her thigh.

"What about him?" Taylor asks.

"He's perfect for Harrison."

"You think?" She raises an eyebrow.

"Yes." I nod firmly, then take a sip of passion fruit seltzer. "I'm going to make that happen."

"What are you talking about?" Georgia asks, brushing her bleached bob behind her ear, leaning forward, waiting for gossip.

"Emmett's a matchmaker now," Taylor says. "He's trying to do for Harrison what he did for me."

"Oh, that is so cute," Georgia says. "Can I play?"

"Well, it's not a game," I say as sweetly as I can. "And I already picked someone out. I just need to get them to hang out a bit. Confirm there's chemistry, and then hopefully one thing will lead to another, and...a second happy couple." I smile at Taylor, who leans into West.

Sure, a second happy couple leaves me without an outlet for physical pleasure, but after a day of evaluating the other queer boys at school, I think I have several who would do as a replacement. Plenty of them would be open to a different kind of relationship, I think.

"Oh, well, that's fun. We should do a group hang with them."

"Agreed," I say. "The winter carnival would be great, but it's too far off. Maybe a movie?"

"Oh!" Georgia says. "We should go to that new pop-up art exhibit at the place that used to be the movie theater? But they renovated it into, like, a performance space?"

"Yeah." Taylor nods. "The projected art thing? It's um...some old artist, William Hodge. He did landscapes in the seventeen hundreds."

"Hodges?" West asks, lighting up. He's an art nerd. Part of why I knew he and Taylor would work so well.

"Yes!" Georgia says. "But they project them in these rooms and they move and there's, like...wind, I think. And at the end there's, like, a virtual drawing room, too. They started in Paris—John went, he said it was so much fun and I had to go."

"That does sound like a good first-date group event," I say, nodding. Georgia might be a bit abrasive, personality-wise, but credit where it's due: it is a good idea.

"John will be so happy we went!" she says, almost shrieking, like she heard me thinking something positive about her and just had to cancel it out. I sigh. She means well. I should be nicer.

"Thanks, that's a great idea," I say, smiling at her. "Now I just have to get Harrison and Clarke on board."

"So this weekend?" West asks. "I love William Hodges, actually. I mean, there's something super colonialist about it, but also it's just...really pretty. I did a report on him for art history this semester. I don't know how I didn't know about this...what is it?"

"An augmented-reality space," Georgia says, reading from her phone. "A full sensory virtual experience putting you in the exotic landscapes painted by William Hodges."

"Don't love the use of the word *exotic*," West says.

"Sights, sounds, smells, and more," Georgia continues. "A vacation for the soul."

"I don't know," Taylor says.

"I'm still up for it," West says. "We can always make fun of it."

"John said it was super beautiful," Georgia says, her voice a little whiny.

"What is?" Miles asks, sitting down next to me. He's holding a half-eaten banana.

"This William Hodge virtual soul vacation thing," Georgia says.

"Hodges," West corrects.

"We're going this weekend," Georgia says to Miles, reaching her hand out toward him. Her nails are bright yellow, and she taps them on the table. "It'll be fun."

"Who's going?" he asks, looking at me.

"Well, us four, and Harrison and Clarke, if I can get them to come."

"Ah," Miles says. He laughs. "Clarke?"

I don't dignify that with a response.

He shrugs. "All right, sounds weird, I'm in."

"Yay!" Georgia clasps her hands together. "This will

be so much fun. And John will be so happy we all took his advice. If this works, though, I'm next. Boyfriend, girlfriend, theyfriend, whatever, maybe all three!"

"I think I'm sticking to one setup at a time, but I'll see about creating a polycule for you after."

"Honestly." She shakes her head. "That sounds like too much work. Just find me a few hookup buddies."

"I'll be on the lookout. And thank you," I say, gracious, "it's a fun idea for a date. Now I just need to wrangle the happy couple."

Harrison is easy. We have a committee meeting for the winter carnival, which of course goes perfectly, and after that I ask him if he needs any tutoring, and we go back to his place. His parents work late, so it's always empty, even if that ceiling fan has been looking at me funny lately.

After, lying in bed, I tell him.

"So what do you think of Clarke?"

"Clarke Hansen? My year?" he asks, looking confused.

"Yeah."

"I mean, I don't talk to him much. He seems cool. Everyone likes him, right?"

"Do you think he's hot?"

"You're asking me that right after what we just did?"

I shrug. "Why not? I'm asking you about romance. What we just did wasn't that."

"I guess," he says, almost sighing, then rolls onto his side, away from me, and sits up. "I mean, yeah, Clarke is hot. He's got that cheerleader body and everything."

"Good. I think you two would be great together."

"So you're really setting me up?"

I sit up, too, resting my hand on his shoulder, and he turns around. "That's all right, isn't it?" I frown. If he doesn't want me to set him up, but does want a boyfriend, then I may have to be unkind. "We did talk about it, and I thought you gave your blessing."

"It's just weird you doing it, I think," he says. He frowns, then lies back down. "No, what's weird is you telling me about it after sex. I think that's it."

"Oh." I lie back next to him. "I'm sorry. I thought it was...fine, I guess? Should we stop having sex if I'm going to be setting you up?"

"Have you asked him about me?" he asks, his eyes widening with anxiety.

"Not yet. My plan is a group hang—we're all going to this virtual art thing this weekend. I figure we invite you, him, Taylor, West, Georgia, Miles..." I manage not to sneer on the last two names. "Makes it feel less like a setup. Then you two have a chance to see if you like each other, and maybe it all happens then, or maybe I give him a little nudge after...we'll see."

"Okay." He bites his lip, which is really hot, and closes his eyes, nodding to himself. "This weekend?"

"Yeah, that okay?"

"Sure. Um, but then...yeah, I feel like we should stop...tutoring. I don't want to get into something with someone else while I'm still...tangled with you."

"We're not tangled," I say. "We're just friends who enjoy each other intimately sometimes."

He laughs. "We have sex, Emmett. And that makes it more than just your usual friendship. More...complicated. Maybe not for you, but for me. So we should stop."

"All right," I say with a sigh. "Well, it's been a lot of fun."

"We should stop...," he says, sitting up and then straddling me, "...after today."

"Even better."

Clarke is harder. We're friendly, sure, but I've never sought him out for anything. He's not on the student council, and he doesn't volunteer at the soup kitchen. He mostly just cheers, I think, and goes shopping and then hangs out at home doing his KamerUhh videos. So the best place to catch him is cheer practice, just after school.

After the string quartet leaves for the day, the school pipes in classical music through the PA system for any students staying late. Today it's a flute solo that gets fainter as I walk away from the main building toward the football field.

The field is regulation-size, just behind the school and next to a cliff that overlooks the ocean. It's really lovely, and the cool December wind breezes through my hair as I approach. Just as the flute fades out, the sound of chanting fades in.

"Highbury Academy! We'll Win the Game Dramatically!"

In the stadium, there's a soccer practice going on, but I follow the cheer chant around it to a large grassy field where the team has set up. They're not in the usual robin's-egg-blue-and-canary-yellow uniforms that make them look like well-muscled Easter eggs; they're just in school gym clothes. I spot Clarke in front of the group. He's in a yellow hoodie with the arms cut off and a pair of blue bicycling shorts with yellow stripes down the side. His legs and ass look amazing. If I were Harrison, I'd be thrilled.

"That's fantastic, Alicia!" he shouts. "Great turn on that. Elisa, give her a little more lift, really extend the arms to match Brittany! Brittany, you're perfect as always! Let's try it one more time!"

I approach quietly and wait for them to go through the routine again, Alicia soaring into the air and flipping before landing perfectly, like a bird.

"That was perfect," Clarke says. "You're all beautiful, amazing people. Amy?"

He turns to his cocaptain, Amy, who nods, then steps

forward. "Now we're going to focus on the rolls! Don, Paul, you're up!"

As Amy takes over the practice, Clarke backs away and picks up a water bottle, then spots me and smiles. He takes a long sip, some water pouring over his lips and running down his chin, which he wipes before walking over to me.

"What brings you out here, Emmett?"

"The squad looks amazing."

"Thanks!" Clarke grins. "Just came to admire?"

"Checking you have everything set for the Cheerleader Dunk booth for the carnival," I say.

"Oh." He nods. "Yep, we're all set. The rental place is going to be there at seven a.m., and I'll be there to make sure it's all done right. You'll be there to make sure it goes in exactly the right spot, right?"

"Of course."

"Then we're set." He takes another drink of water. "That all?"

"Actually, I was wondering. Do you know Harrison Stein?"

"Sure." He nods. "Kinda floppy hair, quiet?"

"That's the one," I say with a nod. "He and I and a few other folks are checking out that virtual art exhibit this weekend. You want to join?"

"Virtual art exhibit?" He raises an eyebrow. "I don't even know what that is."

"Oh," I say, "well—"

"But text me the details. I'll be there for sure." He smiles broadly. "We never hang out. It'll be fun."

"I think so, too," I say, wondering if the *we* he means is him and me, or him and Harrison, or all three of us. "I'll text you. But I'd better get going. I volunteer at the soup kitchen today."

"Oh god, you're so nice," he says, rolling his eyes. "Makes me look bad."

"Don't be silly—you're leading an army of encourage-ment." I gesture at the cheer squad. "Very important."

Clarke glances at them, then turns back to me. His face looks a little pink in the sunlight.

"Yeah, I try. Well, have fun at the soup kitchen. See you this weekend."

"See you then," I say, turning around and walking back to the parking lot. When I can hear the flute again and know I'm safely out of sight, I let myself grin and jump for a moment. This is going perfectly. Clarke and Harrison will be wonderful together.

chapter three

THE SOUP KITCHEN ALWAYS SMELLS WARM. I VOLUNTEER ON Wednesdays, which is the same day Miles and his mom come by. It used to be all of us—him, his parents, my parents. But when Mom died, Dad and I didn't come for a while, and when I said I wanted to start going back, he didn't come back with me. Said he was worried about germs, but I think that's just an excuse. Because it always feels like Mom is there, sort of. Maybe less so since Priyanka went to South Africa. It's all a little emptier. Just me, Miles, and Jasmine now.

"Hi, Emmett," says Izzy, who runs the soup kitchen, when I come in the back. She checks me in on her clipboard and hands me an apron. "Jasmine is cooking…I don't know what. It smells delicious, though."

"It always does," I say, tying my apron on.

"Only on Wednesdays," she says. "I'm going to put you in the kitchen today with Jasmine and Miles, okay?"

"Of course," I say. "Wherever you need me."

"That's what I like to hear," she says, and points me at the kitchen. I leave the staff room and head inside to the large industrial kitchen, where Jasmine is operating the six-burner stove like the pro she is. To one side of the room, her PA, Knight, is filming her on their phone. Next to her, at the counter, is Miles, chopping up carrots.

"Perfect," Knight says, angling the shot so they're getting both of them.

"And here comes another member of our family," Jasmine says, smiling at me. "Grab a peeler and help Miles with carrots, Emmett. We have pounds to get through."

"Sure. Hi, Knight."

"Hey, Emmett," Knight says. Knight is extremely cool. They're a college junior who's been Jasmine's intern for the past two years, managing social media, appointments, all that stuff. Paid, of course. Knight is their nickname, from their having actually saved someone while riding a horse at a Renfaire one time—at least, that's what they say. Their real name is Sam Aquilar, but they never go by it. They're hot, too, in a daddy kind of way, always wearing a leather motorcycle jacket, and with a black beard and a dyed white streak in their hair. I wonder if, once I turn eighteen in a few months, Knight might be amenable to taking over Harrison's current...

well, I don't want to call them responsibilities. Privileges. Though that might be too close for comfort, with them being such a big part of Jasmine's life.

I contemplate it as I grab the peeler and start in on the large pile of carrots next to Miles.

"So how goes it with the great matchmaker?" Miles asks. "Did Clarke, social media maven, agree to being set up with someone who I'm not even sure has a KamerUhh account?"

"He's coming with us to the Hodges exhibit," I say. "But I didn't lead with it being a setup. I said a bunch of us were going, including Harrison. Hopefully they'll just hit it off. It's best to let these things happen naturally."

"Naturally," Miles repeats, a condescending smirk playing on his lips.

"Photos!" Knight says, walking around to us. Jasmine pauses at the stove, turns, and puts her arm around Miles's waist, smiling at the camera. I edge away. "You get in there, too, Emmett," Knight says, waving me closer. Miles puts his arm around my waist and I lay mine on his shoulder, smiling. "Perfect. That is a trio of attractive people helping out." They snap a photo and Jasmine goes back to the stove.

"Emmett, that's enough carrots for now," Jasmine says, glancing over. "Can you chop onions?"

"Sure thing," I say, looking around the kitchen and

finding the onions and preparing for the tears as I start to chop them.

"Knight, you can go for the day, or you can grab an apron," Jasmine says. "That's more than enough social media."

"All right, I have a paper I need to work on, but don't forget you have that call in half an hour to go over the cover for the next book."

"You put an alarm on my phone," Jasmine says, tapping her pocket. "I won't forget."

"There's a new book?" I ask.

"Miles didn't tell you?" Jasmine asks, looking at her son, confused. "It's going to have photos of you in it. You were supposed to tell him for when we ask him and Henry to sign the release." She bumps him with her waist.

"I was waiting," Miles says, looking sheepish. "You only decided on the concept last week."

"Family meals. Mixed families—not just me and Priyanka, southern and Indian, but your mom, too, and some of the stuff I learned from her—Jewish food. Those latkes we made together. And the stuff she and Priyanka used to do in college, and…there's a whole culture of Jewish Indian food, too, but I didn't want to get into that, felt appropriative. So just…family. My family. And that includes your mom, and you."

She pauses as I stare at the onions, remembering the

smell of my mom's latkes suddenly. I realize I should say something.

"That's all right, right?" Jasmine says softly. "If it's not…"

"No, no, that's…" I wipe my eyes from the onions. "That'll be great. You can use whatever photos of me you want, of course. And I can see if I have any of my mom cooking."

"I have plenty of those."

"You do?" I ask. I don't know why that feels a little like a punch. "Have I seen them?"

"Of course you have… but why don't you come over sometime, help me pick the best ones, okay?"

The onions are strong enough that I have to turn away for a moment. "Sure," I say. "Of course I'll help." It's the nice thing to do.

We're quiet as Jasmine adds some of the chopped carrots to the huge pot in front of her. The latkes they made together were a mix of all these different things, and they weren't just for Hanukkah, they were something any of them could have made any time of year. Potato and onion, fried in oil, but also corn, zucchini, chili peppers, all mixed in there, with a little paneer to help bind them, and because Mom always said you had to eat dairy on Hanukkah to honor Judith. They had some cumin and turmeric, too, and grated garlic you had to squeeze when wrapped in paper towels, so it wasn't too wet. They tasted like a hundred different things. I haven't eaten them since she died. I didn't think anyone else had, either.

"You don't have to, you know," Miles says to me, softly so his mom can't hear. "You can tell her you don't want it."

I shake my head quickly. Not let her use a recipe she created with my mom because I'm sad I haven't eaten it since she died? No. "It's what she wants. I'm not so mean I wouldn't let her...and I think it'll be nice. To have that recipe out there. Photos of Mom..."

"You sure? *I* will tell her not to."

"I'm sure," I say. "Thank you. But you really don't need to worry about me, Miles."

"Right," he says, not believing.

"All right, bye, everyone," Knight says, waving at us as they head out the door. "Bye, Emmett. I'll tag you in that photo."

"Sure," I say. "Feel free to DM me, too," I say. "We're going to an art show this weekend. You should join."

"Oh man, I have concert tickets. Maybe next time, though?" They smile as they head out the door.

"Please do not flirt with my mom's assistant," Miles says, his voice a sigh.

"Like I said, don't worry about me." I smile up at him.

"You're crying," he says, suddenly very worried-looking. He turns on his mother. "Mom, I don't think—"

"Miles," I interrupt, like telling a dog to heel. "Onions. It's just onions. I really don't need your protecting."

He looks over at me and nods, his face a little cool. "Right. Fine. I'm going to go work the serving line for a bit. The smell in here is intense."

He puts down the carrots and walks out the swinging doors into the main room, where the food is served.

"Do you need me to move back to carrots?" I ask Jasmine.

"No, no, honey." She's looking out the doors, where Miles just went. "What got into him?"

"I don't know," I say. "Just... Miles."

"I feel like he's been so secretive lately. Is he seeing anyone? A girlfriend?"

"No," I say. "He hasn't had a real girlfriend since Bella in fourth grade. He did call himself a romantic last night, which came as a surprise to me."

"He did take that girl to homecoming last year, what was her name?"

"Shereen. From debate club. He said they were just going as friends, though." I wonder for a moment if Jasmine is onto something, if he has a secret girlfriend. He and Shereen are close but I've never seen a hint of anything romantic between them. Maybe they're special friends like me and Harrison. No, he clearly doesn't approve of that kind of thing. Maybe they were secretly dating but broke up and now he's interested in someone else....Are there any girls I've seen him hanging around with? Eating lunch with? No, it's mostly just been me... oh no. Georgia. I shake my head, banishing the thought. He would never. I'm overthinking this.

Jasmine shakes her head, then turns to another pan on the stove. "Kids your age change a lot, you know. So quickly. I try to keep up but..."

"My father texted you last night when he hadn't heard back from me in five minutes."

"Oh, Emmett, he just worries, it's not—"

"I know. I'm just saying—as parents go, I think you're doing a great job. Whatever is going on with Miles is his to deal with."

She smiles. "All right, so you're saying I'm a good mom as long as I wait six minutes before texting someone when I haven't heard back from him?"

"Essentially."

She laughs. "You're a good kid, Emmett."

I turn and look at the big swinging doors. Through the circular windows in them, I can see Miles standing behind the table where the food is, offering to make a plate for anyone who needs assistance.

"I try to be nice is all," I say, still watching.

When the food is done a while later, I go out and stand next to him, but we don't speak. Instead, I help some of the elderly and food-insecure folks who come in, looking for food and, more often than not, some conversation. I like talking to them, which is mostly listening, hearing them talk about a dead spouse or child or how I look like someone. It doesn't always make sense, they're just happy to have someone to talk to. I ask questions and give them food and I can feel them relax, which somehow makes me relax—not because it's easy or because I'm not doing what I should, but because there's something warm inside me that makes me feel different than I do the rest of the time. Different than nice. Better than nice, whatever that is.

Beside me, Miles does the same thing. When the shift is over and the room clears out, I look at him, and he smiles and waves goodbye without saying anything. I wonder why he didn't tell me about the cookbook. I wave goodbye back.

I decide not to mention the cookbook to Dad when I get home. I think that should be Jasmine's job. He might not take it well, or he might sob, or love it, I'm really not sure. I love my father, but the truth is that since Mom died, it's been hard sometimes. He's not abusive, obviously, and there's nothing I could want for. I'm blessed. I know that. It's just his moods, his worrying. Sometimes it feels bigger. Sometimes it feels like there's an invisible house collapsing that only he can see and only he can hold up, and if he doesn't, we'll all be crushed, but when I ask him to show me how I can help, how we can escape or prop up some plaster, he just starts going on about health, STDs, free radicals....Sometimes it makes me scared. That's why I want to be a doctor, I think. So I won't be scared. Because I'll understand it all. And then I can make sure he's not scared. And make sure people like Mom don't... well. That one is a little obvious, isn't it?

Even before Mom died, sometimes he got kind of anxious about stuff—he spent a month researching bike helmets before he let me get one. I had the bike just sitting in the garage. I think he would have gone longer, but one day when I was asking if I could just get a helmet so he could teach me how to ride, he said no, and Mom wrapped her arms around him, tight, a tight long hug, and she said, "You can't control the world, Henry. He has to live in it anyway." And then he got me a helmet. He taught me how to ride that weekend. Wouldn't take the training wheels off for a year, but I was riding. That's how I think it is with him now—I'm living, just with training wheels, like the lie about sex and sometimes taking my blood. It's weird, I know, but once, the tests did spot a case of bronchitis before symptoms started and I got some preemptive treatment, so it's not all bad, really.

For dinner, Dad makes some kind of superfood pasta that tastes a little like granola but isn't bad if I add enough pesto and drink enough green tea. He talks to me about work—a client of his who is trying to put together a non-profit to create towers that pull pollution out of the sky. He loves the idea, says they sound like reverse volcanoes, but he's sad they don't look as magical as they sound. "They're just towers, Emmett. You'd think they'd add some light effects or cover them in flowers so people understood what they're doing but..." He sighs. "I suppose some things are just practical, and not beautiful."

"Maybe," I say.

"Let's get some flowers from the garden," he says when we're done eating, and we go outside and carefully cut some primroses and hydrangeas and arrange them in vases around the house.

"Maybe the reverse volcanoes can't be as beautiful as they should, but at least our house can," Dad says, kissing me on the forehead as we place the last vase. "I have some papers to review, but I'll be in my study."

"Thanks, Dad," I say, not sure why I'm thanking him. He goes to his study to work and I go to my room to study. I spend the rest of the night reviewing my notes and offering my opinions on jewelry design ideas to Taylor as she sends me sketches and photos. She's spiraling, so worried about this application, and it's my job to make sure she knows how talented she is so she can get it done in time, and get into FIT. I have no doubts about it. Just like I have no doubts about her and me staying friends even if we're on opposite coasts.

She FaceTimes me to show off some new pieces, asking which look best together.

"Does this necklace go with these earrings...or these?" she asks, the camera switching between two sets—one black, one white.

"Show me the necklace with each?" I ask. "Put it next to them."

She obliges, moving the necklace—a multistrand of red metal beads that she handcrafted to look like hearts, but every sixth one is cracking open, a white gold rose bursting out.

"I think the white," I say. "They highlight the roses better." I smile. "Mom loved white roses." Dad says they bloomed for her.

"Oh," she says, quickly turning the camera to her face. "I'm sorry, Emmett, I didn't..."

"I like it," I say quickly. "C'mon, don't do the pity thing with me. You promised."

She smiles, a little sad. "I did, you're right. Sorry."

She never knew my mom. When we were first becoming friends, and I told her about how my mom had died—recently then—I made her promise not to look at me the way the other students and teachers who knew had, like I was such a sad case, poor Emmett. I hated that. It was like cellophane over me, trapping me with my grief. Every "How you doing?" made me have to relive the pain. I couldn't just move on. But Taylor promised, and treated me like any other kid, and that feeling of being normal…it let me be normal again.

"Think she would have liked the necklace, though?" Taylor asks, which for a moment makes my eyes get watery.

"Absolutely," I say.

The camera flips back around and she arranges the necklace with the white earrings.

"She would have loved all your stuff, I think," I say, staring at her hands putting the earrings here, then moving them slightly, draping the necklace differently. "She loved flowers, and you do so many flowers. She didn't wear jewelry much, because it got in the way at work, but studs, she loved little stud earrings. So those white ones would be great."

"But they're not flowers," Taylor says.

"That's okay," I say.

"No," she says. "I have…" The phone gets put down on the desk, the video screen going dark, and I hear her rummaging through her various bins and boxes of pieces she's made. "What was she like?" she calls as she rummages. "That doesn't break the rules, right?"

"I've told you," I say, staring at the photo of Mom on my desk. She's got blond hair, cut very short, but fashionable with longer bangs, and black cat-eyed glasses. Her eyes are bright green. She looks a lot like me, but her chin narrower, pointy, like a pixie. And her smile is so bright and wide. No one could have a smile like that. "She was smart. She always talked about how I wasn't done growing and gave me chances to redo things so that I could grow better. She was forgiving, I guess, but not, like... soft. Just believed in second chances. Growing better. Becoming your best self by twenty-five, I guess. And she had a great laugh."

"I found them," Taylor says, picking up the phone again, the video now focusing on a new pair of earrings— white-gold roses, just like the ones in the hearts. "I'd almost forgotten about these. They were the first thing I made that I really...like, made. It wasn't just an assignment. Think they go better?"

"They're perfect," I say. "My mom would love them."

"Your mom sounds so great," Taylor says, flipping the camera around. "She can even help me out, and I never knew her. Oh no." She sees my face. "I'm sorry!"

"What?" I reach up and touch my face. A few stray tears have leaked out. "Oh, don't worry about it. Just allergies."

"Emmett, you don't have allergies." She smirks. "It's okay to cry when missing your mom."

"I didn't even know I was doing it." I wipe the tears off so my face shows no sign of them.

"Okay...," she says, sounding like she doesn't believe me. "Well, thank you, Emmett's mom, for helping me pick this set out. It's perfect."

I laugh. "She would have loved you, too," I say, and the moment it leaves my mouth it feels like a punch in the stomach, because Mom never knew one of my closest friends. I smile. "What else do you have for the portfolio?"

"Oh, well, I have this messy chaotic multistrand that's like all different flowers...."

We go over her picks for a while more before she says she feels like she's done enough.

"I'll see you tomorrow," she says. "Thank you again. I'm going to give you the best thank-you!"

"Oh?"

"Yeah. Andre, West's brother."

"Taylor, I—"

"Night, Emmett!" She waves into the camera, smiling and ignoring me, before hanging up. I put the phone down and laugh.

I don't know why she's so worried about it, or why she thinks setting me up with West's brother will help, but... well, he is good-looking, and he is at Stanford. It might not be a bad idea to get to know him better.

It's a shame about Harrison's tutoring sessions, though. With midterms, I could use the relaxation, the hormones that make your body calmer, more focused. But none of that is worth having a boyfriend. And setting him up with Clarke is the nice thing to do. He deserves a worthy boyfriend and Clarke is perfect. I'm actually excited for the group hang on Saturday, seeing how they'll click, discover things about each other, flirt. As long as Miles doesn't get in the way, anyway. I can see him doing that, just to show me up, tell me I was wrong.

But no, my plan will work. I will make it work. That's what I tell myself as I get ready for bed. Everything will work out perfectly.

After I've brushed my teeth and washed my face and I'm about to lie down and sleep, I'm struck by a sudden urge and go downstairs, outside into the flower garden. Dad tends it every day, and it smells almost overwhelming as I get close to it, every kind of flower that can bloom letting out a strong perfume, every petal reaching out to touch me as I pass by. It's almost a hedge maze of flowers. But I find the ones I'm looking for, the white roses. They bloom all year round for some reason. Southern California, I guess. I clip one from the stem, carefully, with Dad's pruners, and bring it inside, finding a small vase for it, and then taking it upstairs, where I put it on my desk. It smells so sweet and helps me fall asleep quickly.

Thursday goes by quickly, except for lunch, when Georgia announces she thinks John has a boyfriend in Paris but won't tell her about it.

"I'm happy for him, of course, a French boyfriend is very hot, but it just feels like he's pulling away," she tells me very sincerely. I don't know why she's decided to make me the victim of this conversation. "Having experiences without me. Doing things I haven't done."

"So get a boyfriend," I say. "Or girlfriend."

"I don't want one just because John has one." She sighs. "I want someone I actually like. I just feel…like I'm missing out, you know?" I look around for help, but Harrison and Miles aren't sitting with us today and so the only other people at the table are Taylor and West, who are lost in their own world, giggling at something on his phone.

"I'm sorry you feel that way," I say, not sure what my role here is. "But I'm sure he'll tell you all about it when he's ready."

"We used to tell each other everything." She sighs again and looks down at her own phone. "His last photo of him is cropped. There's a hand on his shoulder. He had to know I'd see it, right?" She holds up her phone. There's John, this time in front of Versailles, a day trip. He's wearing a pendant in the shape of a piano key. "And that necklace is new," she says. "I wonder if it's a gift?"

"Let's not leap to conclusions," I say, trying to reassure her. Georgia is right, though, there's a hand on his arm, like someone pulling him close, but they've been cropped out. "Maybe it's not a boyfriend, just a friend he doesn't want to tell you about yet," I say. "The hand is in a black glove. Could be a woman?"

"Like he has a new best friend?" She looks horrified. "I hadn't thought of that. Oh god."

I think she's about to cry. I sigh. "No, no, just a friend, like, someone he likes; I don't know why I said a woman. Like a boy, who is a friend, but he's not telling you because he doesn't want to jinx it, you know?" I let my mouth twist something out. It sounds reasonable. Though I wouldn't fault him for finding a new Parisian bestie.

"Oh." She nods, the tears not rolling. "That makes sense." She sniffs, probably for effect. "Yes, you're right. He likes a guy but doesn't want to jinx it. Or get me too excited. You know how I get overly excited about things. Romance, couples." She looks over at Taylor and West. "I do love love."

"Sure," I say, taking a sip of my pomegranate-flavored seltzer. "Who doesn't love love?"

chapter four

THANKFULLY FRIDAY GOES BY QUICKLY, THOUGH I THINK MILES might be avoiding me for some reason. It makes the days undeniably more pleasant, but I'm annoyed with him for being annoyed with me and not telling me what he's annoyed about. He's supposed to lord his little moral high grounds over me, not sulk and avoid me in the halls. But, on the bright side, that might mean he won't show up to the art exhibit and try to sabotage my Harrison-Clarke matchmaking.

We have tickets for 1 p.m. on Saturday, so I sleep in and make myself a late brunch of eggs and fruit before driving over to the old movie-theater-turned-exhibition-space. I can't remember what particular brand of cineplex the theater was, but it was huge, with IMAX screens on the second floor. The outside of it hasn't changed much, with an awning with neon lights and those black letterboard signs where the names of movies would go. Now it simply says HIGHBURY ART SPACE. It's a bit minimal. I was expecting at least a new sign, maybe a fresh coat of paint. But the only change is that the glass cases where movie posters used to hang now have posters for the exhibition, and a calendar of upcoming events, of which there is only one besides the Hodges show. Grim.

I'm the first there, and the parking lot is deeply empty, so I study the posters. Landscapes, attractive ones, and promises of an "immersive experience" that will "teleport you through time and space." I suddenly realize I shouldn't have agreed so readily to something suggested by Georgia and praised by John. I was too eager for something intriguing. But this looks like it could just be embarrassing for everyone involved—ticketholders included.

I clasp my hands behind my back and study my reflection in the glass over the poster. No, I decide. Even if the exhibit is tedious, the conversation won't be. At least not for Harrison and Clarke. I'll make sure to keep it lively and entertaining.

Taylor and West arrive a moment later in West's black Lexus LC. It's always fun to see people out of school on the weekend, because no one is in uniform anymore, so their real style shines through. I, not wanting to be a distraction, chose a white polo and salmon-colored khakis, and West is in an oversized T-shirt and jeans, but Taylor is on full display, a gorgeous A-line dress the yellow of the sky at sunset, which shows off her jewelry—a pendant, bangles, earrings. It might be too much on anyone else, but it's perfectly coordinated. The pendant is the focus, a large Star of David in blue and pink triangles, overlapping, and apparently stitched together where they touch, with white blooming vines. In the center is a cameo.

"That is beautiful," I tell her.

"Thanks. The profile is my grandmother. I think it's going to be the cover piece for my portfolio."

"It's really amazing," I say. "Let me see the earrings?"

She tilts her head. "You've seen these." I have. They're beautiful little textured studs in silver, like the moon. "And these," she adds, raising her hand with the bangles, rose gold pressed into what look like blades of grass, wrapped around her wrist.

"I still like looking at them," I say.

"Thanks," she says, but I can tell she's still nervous about the portfolio.

"Relax," I say. "Don't think about the portfolio today. Think about…"

"Hodges," West says. "I'm so excited." He takes her hand and brings it to his lips. "Babe, promise me you'll really look at the art, okay? No stressing."

"I'll try," she says. "I want to."

"I'll help," he says, bending in for a kiss.

I turn away so they don't see me rolling my eyes, and

spot Clarke pulling in. He's got a cute gold Jaguar convertible with vanity plates that read THIGH C, which is also his KamerUhh name. He steps out and he's got on peach short-shorts and a long-sleeved vintage crewneck that reads FLY ATLANTIC and has a woman in a red bathing suit diving on it. He also has on the obscenely expensive jewel-encrusted sunglasses Taylor has shown me ads for. She says they weigh over a pound. Right now she's staring at them.

"Am I late?" Clarke asks, looking at me. "Sorry."

"No, no, we're still waiting on people," I say.

"More?" A corner of his mouth tweaks up for a moment. "Fun."

As if he's summoned her through some unholy ritual, Georgia arrives in her purple Tesla, wearing torn jeans and a plaid button-down—she always wears her school uniform with pants, but I forget how butch she can get in her civvies. Finally, Harrison arrives in his little blue Mini Cooper. I'm a little disappointed by what he's wearing—his jeans should be tighter to show off his figure, and his button-down shirt is tucked in, too formal, kind of nerdy. I should have thought to approve his outfit beforehand. Truth is, I've only ever seen him in his school uniform or his underwear (always black boxer briefs, perfectly acceptable), so I didn't suspect he'd be a bad dresser. And it's not awful, exactly. Still. I smile politely and go to work.

"Harrison, you know Clarke, right?"

"Oh yeah," Harrison says, looking momentarily confused by my introduction. "Hi."

"Hey," Clarke says. I can't tell what his eyes are doing behind the giant crystal sunglasses.

"So let's head in?" I ask. "If nothing else, it'll be a good laugh."

"Oh, come on, it's going to be great," Georgia says. "John loved it."

"What about Miles?" West asks, then turns at the sound of another car arriving. Miles. I guess he just had to show up to ruin this for me. He gets out of the car, in a peach shirt and torn white jeans that do a much better job of showing off his figure than Harrison's do. At least he's straight, so even if he distracts Clarke, it won't lead to anything.

"The parking lot is like a museum exhibit on luxury cars," he says, walking over, a superior little smirk on his face.

"They're all electric, Miles. We're doing a good thing," I say, smiling as brightly as I can at what is obviously him insulting me.

He just smirks again.

"Well, now that we're all here," I continue, keeping my voice from becoming too exasperated, "let's go in."

We show our tickets to a bored-looking college guy running the booth and then go inside. I'm not sure what I was expecting, maybe the lobby I remember from when it was a movie theater, just with art projected on the walls, but now there's a long hallway with a pair of red velvet curtains at the end. The carpeted floor slopes gently up, the walls are black, and there's writing on them in white, with a few paintings and portraits, telling us about Hodges, the painter.

"So we gonna get them to fall in looooooove?" Georgia whispers to me.

"Shhh," I quiet her. Harrison looks over at me strangely.

"He was Captain Cook's painter," West says, looking at the portrait of Hodges on the wall. Everyone is quiet, reading, or at least listening to West. "Cook was supposed to bring a whole team headed by a botanist, but he couldn't build them an extra deck on the boat, so he was assigned some supposedly B-tier academics to explore the islands with him. Hodges was one of those."

"There was just an NPR story about that," Harrison says. "It was about how he was one of the first artistic colonizers."

At the end of the hall, standing in front of the curtains, is someone in full period costume: a sailor from the 1700s. I eye him warily. I'm not a snob, but costumed actors usually mean participation, which never turns out well and is the opposite of creating an air of romance.

"Yeah," West says. "And that's not wrong, but it's also really interesting to see the way British eyes first saw Easter Island, New Zealand, Tahiti, and…made them more British in art. That's the colonization. Like, he made canoes look like gondolas, and framed nature in the English way. I think it's so interesting. We think of colonialization as being about taking over space, forcing people into our culture, but it's also about the ways we perceive other cultures and then express our view of them."

We've made it nearly to the end of the hall. The sailor beams, almost menacing, but thankfully stays silent.

"It's pretty, though," Georgia says, looking up at a large landscape. I hate to say it, so I don't, but I agree. Tall statues, like fingers, rise out of the ground, white and pink stone, and behind them the sky is blue on the left, but dark with clouds on the right. There's a skull by the base of the statues, and silhouettes in the distance. Closer to us, shadows are growing longer. The colors are beautiful, pinks and blues and dark storm gray and deep red. It feels modern somehow, in its colors. I'm not an artist like Taylor, and I only took one art history class, but I know it seems peaceful. Still. And a little sad.

"Pretty is a whole other thing," West says. "Subjective, and shouldn't be judged. At least, that's what I think." He glances at Taylor, who nervously twirls her pendant with the hand not holding his. "Art's value isn't in the eyes of one person, or even a small group, after all." Taylor doesn't seem to hear the way he's speaking directly to her, though.

"I thought this was, like, lasers or something," Clarke says, mostly to me. I walk so that I'm next to Harrison, and he follows, so the two are practically facing each other. "None of this is KamerUhh-worthy."

"I think that's…" I point at the curtain. And the sailor standing in front of it, now saluting us.

"Greetings, travelers," he says in a heavy fake British accent.

"Oh no," I whisper without meaning to. Clarke snorts a laugh.

The sailor ignores us and continues. "Welcome aboard the ship of Captain Cook!" And with that he draws back the curtain, revealing the inside of a boat. Like, actually constructed, not a projection. We all tentatively walk forward, into the ship. It smells like the ocean, and I can hear sea gulls. It seems to be empty, aside from us.

"Okay, this is something," Clarke says. "I should have brought a sailor hat. We could do cute photos in it." He smiles at me.

"Harrison would look good in a sailor hat," I say, nodding at Harrison, who blushes.

"So cute!" Georgia adds. She's definitely making herself part of this.

"Welcome aboard, my fellow sailors!" says the costumed attendant.

"Just no," Clarke says to him. "We're here for the art, not whatever you are, okay?"

"Clarke," I say, glancing at the sailor, who's frowning. "Let's be nice."

"Yeah, we're here for a whole experience, right?" Harrison says. "Hello, fellow sailor."

"The ship has many doors to different lands," the sailor says, though with less enthusiasm than before. He opens his arms wide at the various doors around us. "Explore the depths of William Hodges's adventures and imagination! But only go on deck when you're ready to depart." He points at the stairs heading up. "And feel free to ask me if you need help finding your sea legs." As he says it, the boat seems to tilt slightly.

"Thank you," I tell him, then turn to Clarke. "See? Not so bad."

Clarke laughs. "Let's just see the lasers."

"This is pretty cool," West says. He's spinning, looking around at the actual ship. "He said to go through the doors, right, so..." He walks up to one and opens it. Pink light pours over him. "Nice." He grins and goes inside, all of us following.

Inside is a fairly large room, circular, and glowing, the walls lit up with a projection of a painting. This one shows beautiful pink-and-green mountains in the distance, and people in canoes in the water closer to us. The room smells like the sea and like flowers, and the floor is covered in white sand.

"This seems fun, right?" West says to all of us, but mostly to Taylor, taking her hand.

"Yeah," she says. He pulls her in for a kiss, and as

their lips meet, bright tropical flower petals fall from the ceiling, fans in the room blowing them so they circle around the couple.

"That is so cute," Clarke says. "Think someone is watching and does it when people kiss?" He turns to me.

"I don't know. That would be awfully specific," I say.

"I need to get it to happen to me for a KamerUhh shot," he says, walking over to where West and Taylor are. He looks at the ceiling. "If someone triggers that, I'd like flowers, too!" Nothing happens. "I'll tag this place! I have like fifty thousand followers!"

"Are you sure he's a good match for Harrison?" Georgia whispers in my ear.

"Harrison will bring him down to earth."

Behind me, apparently eavesdropping, Miles chuckles. I frown—I'd forgotten he was here and was happier for it.

"So how do we do this?" Georgia asks. She might be my only ally in all this, so I should use her, I think. Even if she'll probably squeal irritatingly when they finally kiss.

"See, look at his composition," West is saying, pointing at the projection. Taylor and Harrison are raptly listening to him explain the painting. "The way he sets up the actual framing, where things are. That's probably all fake. And he based this—this whole idea of beauty—on English landscape paintings. He made it look more English."

"Harrison, go stand with Clarke," I suggest. "Maybe the petal rain only works if there's two of you."

"The canoes do look more like gondolas," Harrison says, fascinated, and ignoring me.

"Harrison doesn't want to stand with me," Clarke says, pouting.

Harrison glances over, everything we've said apparently catching up to him. "Oh, sorry!" He hops over to Clarke, standing next to him, but not close. They both look up at the ceiling. Nothing happens. I frown.

"Maybe get closer?" I ask, holding up my phone to take a photo.

They inch closer.

"Put your arm around his waist," Georgia says. Harrison nervously puts his arm around Clarke's waist. I smile. It's a start. But still no flower petals.

"The idea of the 'noble savage' was really popularized because of these," West says, pointing at one of the men in the painting. Harrison looks over, clearly wanting to be in the audience of that lecture.

Clarke sighs. "No, no petals." He pulls away from Harrison, who walks over to West. The moment he's on the other side of the room, the petals start to fall, in a shower of color, over Clarke. His phone is out and he's posing for a selfie within moments. Harrison doesn't seem to notice. I sigh.

"Who thought love would be so hard?" Georgia asks.

"Oh my god, that was so fun," Clarke says, walking over to us. "Look." He shows me and Georgia a video of himself smiling as petals fall down around him. "So cute."

"Yeah."

"Great shot," Miles adds, his voice smug. He's so insufferable.

"We should see what's in the other rooms," Clarke says, and is out the door. West is still lecturing Taylor and Harrison. I look over at Georgia. "We need to get them in a room together, without anyone else," I say. "They need to talk. They'll like each other."

"You seem to know a lot about relationships for someone who's never been in one," Miles says, folding his arms.

"Coming from someone who also hasn't been in a relationship...," I say, matching his condescension level. "Are you saying that thinking about what you might want in a relationship, what that might look like, what you might be willing to give of yourself to get from someone else...that thinking about all that means nothing?"

"I...fine. Sorry," he says.

"Plus I know a lot about gay dating from memes," I say, just to annoy him.

He sighs and I grin as West, Taylor, and Harrison walk toward us.

"Clarke went on to the next room," I say to Harrison, who pales slightly and quickly follows Clarke out. We turn to follow him, Miles and I last, but just as we're leaving, a bunch of petals fall on the two of us. I grab one from my hair. It's real.

"This must have quite the budget for fresh petals every day," I say.

"Yeah," Miles says, taking another petal off my shoulder.

We walk back out to the galley and head into the room across from us, where Clarke is already taking photos. This one is the same as the other, but the painting projected on the walls is more of a marsh, though again surrounded by mountains. Two palm trees seem to sway in the breeze—a breeze I can feel coming from somewhere. The floor, also, is grass, but with water on one side of the room.

"Just as I was coming in, it rained," Clarke says. "Like just a light spray. It was so pretty, but I got a little wet."

He points at his shoulders, which are damp with water.

"Oh no, I'm not getting my hair wet," Georgia says, leaving. "Maybe the sailor will give me an umbrella."

"I like rain," Taylor says, putting her arms around West's waist. "And this room is pretty. It's peaceful." She leans her head on his shoulder and as if triggered, a faint mist pours in, and then a light rain showers us. The lights flicker and there's the sound of thunder. West and Taylor kiss. I look over at Harrison, who is staring at Clarke, who is taking a selfie.

"Go get in the photo," I whisper to Harrison. Harrison

takes a few nervous steps toward Clarke but slips on the wet grass and falls on his ass.

"Almost," Miles whispers in my ear. I can hear the laughter behind his voice.

"That's not nice," I say.

"You're right," he says. "But I don't think Harrison or Clarke want this...."

"Harrison wants a boyfriend, and I said I'd find him one—"

"So that it didn't have to be you?" Miles asks, his voice low. I turn to look at him; his face is wet from the rain, which is stopping.

"Because he's my friend," I say.

"See, this is the whole English landscape arrangement again," West says. Clarke is helping Harrison up.

"I slip all the time during rehearsal if the grass is too wet," he says.

"Still embarrassing," Harrison says.

"Oh please," Clarke says. "It's fine. It's fun, right? Art with rain! Look at this video I got." He shows the screen to Harrison, who leans in over his shoulder, their cheeks almost touching.

"See?" I whisper to Miles. He doesn't respond.

They watch the video while West tells Taylor about the way landscapes are set up. Two couples enjoying the work. I walk out of the room, motioning for Miles to come with me. Outside, the sailor is waiting with towels.

"Well, that's thoughtful," I say.

"Sometimes a real squall can rise up in that cabin," he says, terrible accent at full force.

"I guess so," I say, drying myself off.

"You got them alone with the other couple," says Georgia, who apparently has just been waiting for us. "Think it'll work?"

I shrug. "I hope so." But as I say it, Clarke comes out, Harrison not with him.

"Let's do this one next," he says, pointing at a nearby door.

"Should we wait for Harrison?" I ask.

"Oh, he's fine. West is talking about English composition or something, so he's enthralled." Clarke pauses. "Are you two like…" He points at me, his finger waving vaguely between me and the room Harrison is still in.

"No." I laugh—he's checking that Harrison is single. That's good. "We're just good friends."

"And Emmett tutors him," Miles says next to me. I don't have to look at him to feel the smirk.

"Okay, cool," Clarke says.

I'm about to suggest that if he likes Harrison he should ask him out, but at that moment, Harrison emerges, followed by West and Taylor.

"See, this is what's so interesting about him. It's the kind of colonialism we don't talk about, the propaganda that no one realized was propaganda. Here's how these beautiful countries look, different, but still British. Still ours. I hope they have some of his Indian works. Those were after Cook, but same vibe, for sure. Making these places look like they already belonged to the British."

"Also how the British looked at the world, right? Like it was just there for the taking?" Taylor asks. "But it is insidious to see it like this and hear you talk about it."

"*Insidious* is the perfect word," West says. "Wanna see the next one?"

"Yeah," she says. They go into the next room, and we all follow them. This one has a beautiful water scene depicted on it, like we're in a lake and staring at a building with steps right down to the water, flanked by trees in green and brown, the domed tops of buildings in the distance. The floor here is glass, and underneath is actual running water.

"This is from his India period," West says, nodding. "See how it looks like a little country house on the river, but it's a whole city made of stone." He holds his hand out, and then the leaves begin to fall, green and brown. I look over at Clarke and Harrison, but Clarke is taking selfies and Harrison is looking at the water.

Georgia hip-checks Harrison, nearly sending him into Clarke, who dodges and laughs.

"This is so fun, right?" he says to Harrison. "Here, catch a leaf." He turns the camera on Harrison, who looks confused for a moment but reaches out and snags one.

"Great," Clarke says. "I'll tag you. What are you on KamerUhh?"

"Oh, um…Harrisonofagun," Harrison says. "I made it when I was younger, I should change it."

"It's cute," Clarke says. "There: tagged, followed."

I smile and nod appreciatively at Georgia, who nods back, then clasps her hands together and jumps in place, ruining it. But at least we're making some progress. Clarke following Harrison is practically him sending flowers.

As we walk out and to the next room, Taylor takes my arm and lays her head on my shoulder. "You think I'll ever have an interactive art show dedicated to my stuff?" she asks.

"Absolutely," I say.

She laughs. "How are you so sure? How are you so sure about everything?"

"Things can happen suddenly—and with finality," I say. "If you're not sure about what you want, what you'll do to get it…then when something you don't count on happens, you…I think you can break a little. So you have to be sure. If you get lost in the minutiae of what could go wrong, or what happened that you weren't prepared for… you're lost. You can't stray from the path, you know?"

"Emmett…," she says, squeezing my arm. She opens her mouth, then closes it again. "I feel like I can see so many possibilities—like when I'm working in the wax; it can become anything if I use my hands right. But stuff like this…college, futures…I don't know how to sculpt that. How do you know I'm going to carve something brilliant out?"

"Because you're brilliant, and you know what you want, and you're going to do everything you can to get it. You just need to forget the other possibilities you're seeing. If you get caught up in second-guessing yourself, then you'll lose sight of that. So I will always be here to make sure you don't do that. I'm certain enough for both of us."

She squeezes my arm again and is quiet for a moment. We pause outside the room as the others go inside. "What would an interactive jewelry exhibit even look like?" she asks.

"Oh, I don't know. It'll be the future. Maybe we can try on the jewelry holographically."

"Put yourself in a 3D-printed cameo necklace."

"That's a great idea."

"Actually," she says, turning to go into the room, "it is…."

The next room is freezing cold. Which makes sense as the art around us is ships on an ocean, surrounded by icebergs. The floor isn't slippery but looks like ice, and there's the sound of waves as everyone shivers, looking around. Somehow, impossibly, it starts to snow. I catch a flake in my hand and hold it, but it doesn't melt. Glitter. There's never real snow in Southern California. Except in the mountains, but Dad doesn't like us going that high up because he's afraid the transition to thin air pressure might give us altitude sickness.

I throw the glitter down, a little disappointed. I like snow. At least, I like pictures of it. I've never seen real snow, aside from, like, the fake stuff they spray at the winter carnival. I know, you'd think I'd at least have gone skiing, but Dad is a homebody, and when we do take a trip, he always insists we go somewhere where flowers are blooming...and with a "healthy temperate climate," and "not much risk of catching disease"—London in summer, Paris in spring, Barcelona in fall. And he's never okayed me traveling without him. Last year, Taylor tried to sneak me out and drive up to Big Bear, just to make snow angels, but there was a traffic accident that caused a major delay and we had to turn around before Dad got suspicious.

So I've never seen actual real-life snow. It always looks so pretty in photos. It looks pretty in this painting projected on the walls, too, soft white icebergs like marshmallows or whipped cream on the ocean. I wish it were the real thing.

"He painted from the boat, too," Harrison says. "So this is...Arctic...or Antarctic waters...right?"

West nods, hugging himself. "It's pretty." He looks over at Taylor, who walks closer, and he wraps his arms around her to keep her warm. It's cute, so I try not to roll my eyes.

"How did they get it so cold in here?" Miles asks. "It must be so bad for the environment."

"Good for cuddling up, though," Georgia says, smiling mischievously at Harrison. She's not subtle, but he gets the hint and goes to Clarke.

"Want a hug for warmth?" he asks Clarke. Bold. That's more like it.

Clarke laughs and gives him a hug. Not as tender as I'd like, but at least it's touching. Brief, though, before Clarke skips out of the room.

"Almost snow, right?" Miles says as we're walking out. "You don't want to stay longer?"

"I forgot I told you that," I say, rolling my eyes.

"That you want to see snow? It's not a secret, is it?"

"No," I say, leaving the room. "Just…it's not snow. It's fake. Glitter. I want the real thing." More glitter tumbles down on us and I sigh.

He laughs. "One day," he says, brushing it off my shoulders. So condescending.

I walk quickly to the next room, which is an interior, surprisingly. The painting that wraps around the circle of the room seems to be a large, roofed plaza, with almost Roman columns and doors, people in nineteenth-century dress walking among them, and above, a large domed ceiling, with a single hole in it. The ceiling of the room itself is domed, so it matches the art, and with a hole that light falls through, almost blindingly, creating a spotlight on the center of the tiled floor. The room sounds like footsteps and people chattering in English accents, but faint enough that I can't quite hear them.

"Dramatic," Clarke says happily, immediately standing in the center of the room under the light. He holds his phone up and tries a few angles, then shakes his head. "Too dramatic up close. Hey, Harrison, could you snap a few photos of me?"

"Oh, sure," Harrison says, shooting me a grin before taking the phone from Clarke's outstretched hand. Suddenly Georgia is next to me, grabbing my wrist and clutching it tightly as we watch Clarke pose under the spotlight while Harrison snaps pics.

"I think we're doing well, right?" Georgia asks.

"Yes, because as we all know, cameraman and boyfriend are practically the same," Miles says on her other side.

"It's the gay version of holding your wife's purse," I say.

"I think I'd want to be more than a purse rack," Miles says.

I look over at the two of them, Clarke posing, doing splits, as Harrison keeps snapping. They're both smiling.

"I think if you really loved someone, you wouldn't mind it," Georgia says, surprising me. "Right?"

I look at Miles, who looks surprised, too.

"You might be right," he says.

Suddenly the murmuring noise shuts off and is replaced with the sound of a string quartet, and doors slide open in the walls. Two couples, in full Regency dress, emerge from the wall, already clasped together and dancing to the music. Everyone immediately gets out of the way, watching them dancing in circles around the beam of light, where Clarke still stands, watching, smiling. He catches me looking and grins wider, pointing at the dancing couples and then rolling his eyes. I look over at Harrison, who's watching the couples with a different sort of smile. He's actually enjoying it. Of course he is.

I look back at the dancers, moving perfectly in time, practiced. West takes Taylor and tries to join them in the circle around the center of the room, and though they're less elegant, the way they look at each other is open in a way the dancers aren't.

"I wish I had someone to dance with," Georgia says, sighing. "It looks like fun."

"I'm sure you will soon," Miles says, which makes me frown. It's almost flirtatious, and Miles and Georgia together would be awful. Though maybe it would take them both out of my hair.

"Get photos!" Clarke says to Harrison, who's too busy watching the dancers to realize it's directed at him, so I go over and poke him, motioning to him to take photos of Clarke in the center as the dancers frame him and he takes dancing poses. He looks good. I know it's crude to judge every man I meet on if I'd like to take him to bed, and I don't usually, but sometimes, it just strikes you. The way Clarke moves. The way his shorts hug his thighs. If I weren't setting him up with Harrison, I'd consider him as a replacement.

A moment later, the music fades and the dancers go back into the wall, like cuckoo-clock figures.

"That was great," Harrison says.

"Did I look good?" Clarke asks, coming over to take his phone back and looking at the pictures. "Oh yeah, this is great. You're the best, Harrison. I should keep you around for all my photos."

I look over at Miles and smile. Sometimes being a camera *is* close enough to being a boyfriend, at least at first, right? But he's just glaring at me like I did something wrong. I sigh and lead the others out of the room and back to the ship, and then across to the next room. I almost gasp when I enter it, though, it's so striking.

In the center of the room, hanging as low as my knees, is an elaborate floral arrangement, like a chandelier. Dad would love it. The room is white except for one space where the painting is projected. It's of a castle, and in front of it are a horse and cart, a man driving it, though we can't see his face. To the side, a woman looks over her shoulder, back at them. But the focus is the horse, white, with a black mane, about to cross the bridge. I look at the horse. He seems to be going toward the woman, who stares back with some affection, like she's waiting for him to catch up. But still the horse looks...

"Lonely," Miles says, next to me.

"What?" I ask, annoyed. "There are seven of us."

"I meant the horse," he says, almost laughing at me.

"Oh..." I look back at the horse. "Yes. But look, people are waiting for him." I point at the woman, patient, her head turned back, smiling.

"This is Ludlow Castle," West says. "One of his English pieces. Very classical composition. So, like, he arranged the paintings he did of the islands to look more like this, see?" He's talking to Taylor, but Harrison is listening again, while Clarke takes selfies in front of the floral chandelier, Georgia getting into some of them. So much for helping me out with the matchmaking.

"The castle is a ruin," I say to Miles, trying to tease him.

"This is my favorite room so far," he says, genuine. "It's so beautifully done—look at the way the castle is ancient but still there, the way it makes everything around it seem like they're aware of time, aware of how young they are in comparison to everything...but none of them are looking at the castle."

I stare at the castle again, seeing what he means. Time moves on, but it also stretches out forever.

"I wonder why they put the flowers in here," Taylor says. "There aren't flowers in the painting."

"It's the light," I say. "The light in this painting is, like, flower light."

"Flower light?" Miles asks, his tone so condescending I want to slap him.

"Yes, it's warm, and it feels like the sun," I say, pointing at the painting.

"Flower light," Miles says, smiling, locking eyes with me. Suddenly, flower petals, in red, yellow, and orange, all fall from the ceiling, everywhere. They feel soft as they land on my neck and arms, and raise goose bumps, but I stick my chin up, triumphant.

"Flower light," I say, hands on my hips.

Miles laughs, turning his face up to watch the petals fall. "Yeah, I guess so."

Clarke is taking a photo with Georgia and Harrison, and West and Taylor of course are kissing, but I look at the painting, and the horse and the woman, and let the flowers fall on me. They seem to keep coming, and I look up to see if the machine throwing them down is broken, but I see Miles, staring at me.

"What?" I ask.

"You have one…" He reaches out and plucks an orange petal from my hair.

"You have several," I say, looking at him. He laughs, and for a moment, something feels different, older, or maybe newer, and then the flowers stop, and Clarke stops taking photos and instead walks to the door.

"Let's go see what's on deck," he says, leading us out, and then up the stairs of the ship, onto the deck. I hear him gasp as he reaches the top. And when we all get there, I can see why. Whereas every room before wasn't small, they felt contained; the curved walls with the projected art felt like boundaries. Up here, it seems they've put some kind of dome over the entire space, and it's far out enough that the night sky projected on it feels real. The upper deck of the ship is as well made as the lower, too, so it actually does feel like we're on a ship, rocking, sailing in the night. There's a breeze, and when I look over the side, there's water. It's still, not waves, but it's very realistic. It feels like we're suddenly in another world.

The railings of the deck and the mast have all been decorated with garlands of flowers, too, pastel petals, the stems and vines barely visible under the blooms. When I approach them, they smell and feel real, too, their scent mingling with the smell of salt water, which they must be pumping in through the fans. It's quite the illusion.

And then, to top it all off, in the center of the deck is a string quartet, all dressed as sailors. I recognize the cellist as the one from school. They're playing what I'm almost sure is Lil Nas X's "Montero," which is perhaps the main thing that makes it feel like we haven't gone back in time but is also splendid.

"You may approach the ship's wheel," says the actor who first let us in. He's followed us above deck and gestures grandly at the wheel at the end of the deck. The bow? I don't know. We walk up to the wheel, which isn't really a wheel, as it turns out, but more of a frame in the shape of a wheel. The center of it is a large screen, and the spokes of the wheel pull out—they're brushes and pens, the kinds for touchscreens. Georgia reaches out and taps the screen, and it turns on, showing a sky similar to the one above us, but with menus underneath. She taps the one labeled BACKGROUNDS and a whole slew of backgrounds pop up—from the paintings downstairs, or blank colors, or other landscapes that look like things Hodges painted. She taps the one that looks like a beach scene, and suddenly the stars around us change to that scene.

"No way," she says. She taps another menu, labeled PAINTS, which opens an array of colors. Taking one of the brushes, she taps it in the purple, then on the screen. She paints a heart in the sky, and one appears above us.

"Oh wow," Taylor says, her eyes going wide. "Imagine all the things we can do...."

For the next hour, as the string quartet continues to play pop hits from the past decade, we paint. There are stamps, too, so we can take trees from one Hodges painting and plop them in another: palms on icebergs, flowers falling from the sky, and they appear around us. Taylor and West work on using these to decolonize his paintings, rearranging things into new landscapes for us to pose in front of.

It's amazing the way it projects behind us—like we're suddenly empowered to alter our own world. Taylor of course is the most skilled of us, creating cameo portraits of us to stand in front of, like they're wearing us. West assembles a beach scene. I make the sky blank and tell Harrison to hold still while I paint him in the sky. I'm not an artist, but it looks kind of like him, and when I'm done, Clarke takes a selfie of the three of us—him, me, and Harrison, with Harrison in the stars behind us.

"This is going to be my new lock screen," he says, and I turn to Harrison and see him blushing but happy. Lock screen is definitely a success.

Eventually, we finish drawing in the sky, and we leave the way we came in, the light outside strangely dim after all the bright screens and virtual paintings. I'm hoping Clarke might ask Harrison out before he goes, but instead, everyone just sort of hugs each other before getting in their cars. But when I get home I see I have a text from Harrison:

I really like him

And I smile. Making love happen. What's nicer than that?

chapter five

Inside, Dad is pacing nervously, and the box of holiday decorations we keep in the garage is out. It's early, but he tends to get restless around the holidays. Dad is Episcopalian, but Mom was Jewish, and he tries to make sure we still have Hanukkah this time of year.

"Emmett!" he cries out when he sees me come into the living room. He's holding a large menorah. "Good. Do you know when Hanukkah is? We didn't miss it, did we?"

"You can just ask your phone, Dad," I say.

"The phones are made for Christians," he jokes.

I sigh and look up Hanukkah on my phone. I'm pretty sure it's the end of December this year. "First night is Christmas Eve," I say, nodding.

"Oh," Dad says, staring at the menorah in his hand. It was Mom's, and her dad's before that. It might go back further than that. And he's waving it around the room, looking for a place for it. I sweep forward and gently take it from him, putting it in the window, where it always goes.

"Right," Dad says, looking at it. "Well, we'll have Jasmine, Priyanka, and Miles over that night, then, same as for Thanksgiving."

"It's Christmas Eve, they might want to just be them that night," I point out. Then I think of Mom's latkes in Jasmine's cookbook, and I hope they'll come over. Maybe I *should* tell Dad about it.

"We'll invite them anyway."

"I think Priyanka is back next weekend. They'll be at the winter carnival, so you can ask them there," I say, poking at the holiday decorations box. There's a little stethoscope tree ornament I made.

Dad reaches into the box, too, and pulls out a dreidel. It's glass, not usable, just a decoration. There's a chip in the corner. "Your mother and I got this for our first Hanukkah living together," he says softly. "The chip is from spinning it off the box we were using as a table because we didn't have furniture yet."

He stares at it for a moment, and I don't say anything. I don't know what to say.

He looks up at me and frowns, the grief shifting over, as it often does, to anxiety. "You're being smart, right? Sex is so dangerous, Emmett. Cervical cancer is a result of unsafe sex practices."

"That's not exactly right, Dad," I say.

"You need to be careful!" He sounds so sad. "If you're not careful, it could be over for you, too. I can't let that happen, Emmett. You have to promise me—be safe." He gets closer and holds my arms tight against my body.

"Dad." I swallow. "I promise. That hurts."

"Sorry," he says, letting go. I give him a hug.

"Maybe we should do that blood test?" he asks, hugging me back.

"I need to study," I say, pulling away and heading quickly upstairs.

"Later, then?" Dad calls after me.

I stop in front of my bedroom door and take a deep breath, ignoring him. I know he's been getting worse, so I think ignoring him is the best thing to do, otherwise he'll just dwell on his fears more. It's probably because I'm going to college soon. Or maybe because Priyanka has been gone for a while—having a doctor he could text at any moment who would talk sense into him was good for counteracting whatever medical fear he'd read on the internet that day. Pri will be back soon. I'll be at college. I hope someone will be able to take care of him when I'm at college.

I go into my room and pull out my books. It's only like five, and though I am blessed with a fine intellect, I still require constant studying. Especially if I'm going to go to one of the top med schools in the country, and after that into bioresearch. Vaccines. I want to make a vaccine for cancer. All cancer. Theoretically, it can be done—they already have a vaccine for lung cancer in Cuba. I know I won't be the only one working on it, some savior who comes along and magically makes everything work. But I want to be part of that team. I want to know I did everything I could. So I study, a lot.

I spend the next few hours working on papers and preparing for midterms, which start a week from Monday, right after the winter carnival. Then we go right into holiday break, and I can relax for a while. Pity I won't have anyone to relax with. I suppose I could discreetly ask around school, but I won't have time. You'd think Harrison could have waited until January to start catching feelings. But it's better he told me sooner than later. I like him and would have hated having to break his heart.

And there's always West's brother. Taylor is so keen on setting us up, maybe that'll work out for a brief holiday fling. She doesn't have to know it's purely physical.

I stretch, hungry and tired of studying, and I meet eyes with the stuffed rabbit on my shelf. I feel like it's judging me, but I'm not sure for what.

When I go down for dinner, Dad is cooking, but unusually for him, it smells like something frying—frying is definitely not healthy. I walk slowly into the kitchen, where he's in front of the stove, a pan of latkes in front of him. Mom's latkes. The ones Jasmine is putting in her cookbook. Only, these are looking very burned.

"Damn, damn, damn," Dad says, trying to flip one with a spatula, but it's stuck to the pan. "Damn," he says again, and manages to peel it off, but with so much force it goes flying over his shoulder, toward me. I manage to dodge before boiling oil and potato hit me in the face.

"Careful," I say.

Dad turns, surprised. "I didn't know you were there," he says, suddenly looking guilty. "You weren't supposed to see..." He spins back around and turns off the stove. "Well, I've ruined it anyway."

"What are you doing?" I ask.

"Jasmine called me. Told me about a new cookbook. Has your mom's latkes in it. The ones she and Priyanka made in college, you know?"

"Yeah," I say, my stomach suddenly heavy. "I was going to tell you, but—"

"Oh, don't worry, don't worry," Dad says, waving his hands. He sits down at the kitchen table with a sigh. "I felt sad at first, but then I realized I don't have that recipe. Your mom made them every year. Jasmine, too, of course, but you and me, we just sat in the living room. Sexist, really, letting the women cook."

"It was their thing," I say.

"Yes..." Dad looks over at the dining room table, like he can picture us. "Well, I thought maybe I could do it, so I told Jasmine I'd like the recipe, and asked if I'd have to buy the book to get it, and she said of course not and emailed it to me. So I thought...I wanted to practice. So you and me could make them for Hanukkah this year."

"Jasmine might come over," I say. "I'm sure she could—"

"I wanted *us* to make them." He sighs and rubs his temples.

"Dad." I walk over to him and hug him tightly around the shoulders. "It's okay. We'll learn from Jasmine."

"I should have learned from *her*."

"You will."

"No, I mean your mother. I should have...known more. So I could remember it for you."

"It's fine," I say. "We can figure it out."

"Every morning when I wake up, I still forget," he says. "Still. Years. I expect her to be next to me...." He puts his face in his hands and starts crying.

I feel the same as him. Every morning, I wake up and still get confused for just half a breath—why is it an alarm, the sunlight, Dad knocking on the door—and not Mom kissing my forehead? That's what she used to do. Already dressed for work, smelling of lime. I'd wake up and her eyes would be the first thing I'd see, and her smile. "Time to get up, honey." And she'd squeeze me around the shoulders and then go downstairs to make a quick breakfast for me before going to work. She was the doctor, but she didn't worry about the healthy food. We had eggs, pancakes made with plain white flour, waffles topped with whipped cream. The kitchen used to smell more like sugar, I think. Now it smells like green tea.

I almost want to sob along with Dad, but then we'll both just be sitting here crying, and that's not what Mom would have wanted. She'd want us happy. I know that. So instead, I sit down next to him, and take out my phone and pull up the ordering app.

"Want to order tacos? We can do the new vegan one."

He keeps crying.

I never want to be like this. I don't think less of him for it. I know why he cries. I knew my mother fourteen years. He knew her a lot longer. She was his life. And all he has left now is me. Not nearly enough and nowhere near fair. I never want to feel that.

I go through the app myself, pick out the least disgusting of the tacos, and order more than we'll ever eat. Then I reach out and take Dad's hand and hold it as he cries, waiting.

I'm only a little annoyed on Monday to learn that Clarke didn't ask Harrison out immediately. After all, Clarke is the play-it-cool type. He'll probably bump into Harrison in the hall a few times, do some drive-by flirting, really make sure he won't get a no before committing. Maybe Friday, for the winter carnival. And if not by then, he must just need a little more encouragement, which the carnival will absolutely provide opportunity for me to give him.

"You sure he's going to ask me out?" Harrison says, sitting next to me at lunch.

"Yes," I say. "I'm going to make it happen." I'm eating a plum and take a napkin to wipe the juice from my chin.

"People are complicated," Miles says, immediately raining on the parade. "We don't know how they'll act, but you're a great guy, Harrison."

"People aren't complicated," I say, taking a swig from the water bottle of green tea Dad insisted I take to school. "They feel things, they act on them. We simply have to make him feel desire for you, and the museum was an excellent first step. Look, he's even staring at you."

I glance up and look a few tables over, at the cheerleaders. Clarke is definitely facing our way. He smiles. Outside, the string quartet is playing, and the music drifts in, sonorous and sweet.

"See?" I say to Harrison. "Just make sure he knows you're interested. Smile back."

Harrison smiles broadly, horrifyingly. The cellist in the quartet hits a sour note, as if they've spotted him.

"Not like a possessed clown," I say, quickly leaning in front of him so he can't see Clarke and Clarke can't see him.

"Sorry," Harrison says, sighing. "I got nervous and forgot how to smile."

"Right," I say, as sweetly as I can. "Well, practice in the mirror later."

"Table poll!" Taylor says across from us. "My portfolio needs a cover. I have it down to two—which do people like?" She holds out her phone, swiping between the options. Both feature her Star of David cameo necklace draped over velvet, but in one, the velvet is black and her name is in white, and in the other, the velvet is a neon pink with black cheetah spots and her name is in black.

"Pink," I say.

"That was decisive," Miles says. "I like them both."

"So do I," I say. "I just like the pink better. It's more youthful."

"I think it's a bit out there," Harrison says. "I like the black."

"This is how you repay my setup efforts?" I ask with an arched eyebrow.

"I like the pink," Georgia says. "Want me to send them to John and see what he thinks?"

"No," Taylor says. "Thanks, but I need to decide by the end of the day. West likes the black. So, Miles… you're the deciding vote."

"I think it's about context," Miles says. "They're both beautiful, but they have different vibes. What vibe do you want the school to think you have?"

"Context?" I ask, keeping the skepticism out of my voice.

"Sure. Context is king. Did you just block Harrison from smiling at Clarke because you were stopping Clarke from seeing a horrifying smile—"

"Was it that bad?" Harrison asks.

"—or," Miles continues, "were you doing it because you don't want them together?"

"Obviously I want them together. It was my idea."

"Clarke might not know that," Miles says with a smile. "He doesn't have the context. It's what helps you determine if someone is a friend or future boyfriend or whatever else, right? You told me yourself it's complicated when you're queer."

I sigh. "Fine. Context. But we don't know it. We don't know what the portfolio judges will be looking for."

"What do they say they're looking for?" Miles asks, taking out his phone. He brings up the website for FIT. "They want something that shows your unique self-expression and special quirks."

"Is that an academic term?" West asks, grinning. Taylor elbows him.

"So?" Taylor asks. "That's your context, your vote is…"

"Pink," Miles says, frowning as he says it. "Though I'm sure—"

"So I was right," I say. "Without all the context."

"The context is what makes it right," Miles says. "Black is what most jewelry is displayed on. Pink leopard print is unique."

"I was right," I say again, smiling.

"You were right," he says, shaking his head.

"Is this smile okay?" Harrison asks, spreading his lips again.

"Oh, honey," Georgia says for all of us. "No."

I know the rest of the week is going to be busy: final preparations for the winter carnival, studying for midterms, and trying to orchestrate Clarke asking out Harrison. But the most important thing is Taylor's portfolio. We go over it again on Monday night, and again on Tuesday, which is pushing it, before she finally sends it in after school.

"It's ready, right?" she asks me and West, who are both there. "It's good?"

"It's amazing," I tell her.

"Babe. It is so good," West says, taking her hands. "That last piece you did after the museum. And your essay? It's amazing. If you don't get in, that's not because of you, it's because they're bad judges."

"You think I won't get in?" she asks, her eyes going wide and watery.

We're sitting in her room, where she's just hit submit on the computer. Her hands are shaking, so I reach out and take one.

"You're going to get in," I say. "You're going to go to New York and make jewelry for celebrities and be famous."

She stands to hug me, and I get up and hug her back, tackling her backward onto her bed with a laugh. "Thanks, Emmett. I'm glad you're always here to be confident when I'm not."

"It's an honor and a privilege."

"And you—" She turns on West and kisses him on the mouth. I politely look away, even though they're directly next to me now. "Thank you."

"That's what boyfriends are for, right? And it's going to be awesome. You'll be at FIT, I'll be at NYU studying art history... it's going to be great."

I turn to interrupt, but as they gaze into each other's eyes, suddenly, through the open window, a flurry of dandelion seeds blows in, crowning them with a mist of white pollen.

"Oh for god's sake," I say, getting up. "These botanical flurries were cute at the museum but now they're becoming absurd." They don't even seem to hear me, but they kiss again, and then an alarm goes off on West's phone and he takes it out of his pocket to shut it off.

"We'd better get going," he says to her, and she nods, then turns and sees me, and looks suddenly guilty.

"West got us reservations at BRUISE, that new vegan place in the city," she says. "I bet if we show up and ask for another chair, though—"

"I don't know if that's right, babe."

"No," I say quickly. BRUISE is very fancy. He clearly

has a romantic celebration planned, and I won't interrupt that—it wouldn't be nice. Even if I had sort of counted on spending more time here. "I won't interrupt your celebration. Have fun and let me know how the food is."

"I'll send you photos," she says, putting on a jacket and pecking me on the cheek. We all walk out together, and I get into my car, watching them get into West's car in my rearview. They kiss before they drive off, and Taylor waves at me as they pass. I start my car up and pull away, heading home. I need to go over all my notes for the winter carnival anyway. There are vendors to follow up with, and booth placements to confirm—so much to do, I'll be busy all night. And Taylor gets to send in her portfolio and then have a romantic night out, which is everything I want for her.

The rest of the week goes quickly—maybe too quickly. Between studying and preparing for the carnival and helping Taylor sort out the guest list for her party during winter break, the one for West's brother, Andre, there's too much to do to really focus on Clarke and Harrison. Though, on Wednesday, Harrison texts me to report that Clarke said hi to him in the hallway and he said hi back. And by Thursday night, I feel so energized that I practically decorate the entire school campus for the winter carnival on my own. Of course everyone else on council helps, but I'm the one telling them where to put up the beautiful handcrafted oversize stars we've strung with white twinkle lights, which are the focal point of the decor. Everything is white. White lights, white fake snow, white booths. Looking at it by the time we're done, in the dark, it honestly almost makes me believe a snow flurry hit the school grounds and everything is the winter wonderland I've always dreamed of seeing.

"It looks great," says a voice next to me as I survey the landscape. I turn to my right, and there's Robert, nodding at the field. "You have an eye for this, Emmett."

"Thank you," I say graciously, because let's be honest, he's understating it. The natural flow of the booths, from the entrance, where the tickets are bought, flowing through the games, to the rides at the back, with the charity booths scattered between them, so they feel like part of the fun—it's excellent.

"Do you think we need trees?" I ask him. "Fake pines or something? I'm sure the school has some in storage."

"Well—"

"I think just one. Can you go get it? A big one. We'll put it in the center. No decorations or anything on it, don't want it to become too ecclesiastical."

"I don't think that's quite what the word—"

"You know what I mean. Winter, not Christmas."

"Sure," Robert says, "I'll go check." He trots off and I look at the landscape again. I'll have to turn the lights off before we go, but right now it glows. I almost feel chilly looking at it, even though it's only sixty degrees and I'm in my school jacket and sweater.

"Hey, Emmett," Harrison says, approaching me. "We've chalked off the spaces for the ice-cream truck; it'll be front and center."

"Yes, I can see it all in my mind's eye. We're going to put a fake tree behind the truck."

"Cool."

"Anything new from Clarke yet?"

"Uh…no. I texted him, though. Like an hour ago."

"Oh?" I look away from the landscape and focus on Harrison. We did not discuss this. He's staring at his feet. "What did you text him?"

"Hey."

"'Hey'?"

"Yeah, that's what I texted him—hey."

I swallow and turn back to the landscape. Everything there is perfect. Or will be once we have the tree.

"I know," he says. "It's not great."

"No, it's not," I say. "But it'll be fine. Everyone is awkward sometimes."

Harrison's phone beeps, and he takes it out of his pocket, then smiles. "He texted back."

"Yeah?" I ask, excited. Maybe this will work out.

"He says, 'Hi, Harrison! Is everyone going to be at the carnival all weekend?'"

"He wants to know if you'll be there," I say, excited now. "That's good."

"Yeah." Harrison is beaming. "What do I say back?"

"Just tell him yes, and you'll be sure to stop by the dunking booth."

He types painfully slowly, each key click noise a heavy footstep, and then hits send. We wait, breathless. The phone dings again.

" 'See you there,' " Harrison reads.

"Did he add the splash emoji?" I ask, looking over his shoulder.

"No," Harrison says. "Is that bad?"

"It would have been flirty, but it not being there doesn't mean anything. He could be keeping it classy."

"Do I say anything back?"

"No," I say. "Just wait until tomorrow."

Harrison swipes his messages closed and I look back out at the winter wonderland we've created. There's an inflatable snowman to one side of the entrance, and I'm not sure I like the look of him. Maybe he should be farther in. Obviously, we have to have a snowman, I just wish we had one that looked like it was actually made of snow.

"Should we move the snowman?" I ask. Harrison doesn't respond. I look over at him. He's opened KamerUhh and is watching a video of Clarke doing a bouncing split and dance routine in time to, I think, one of Holst's *Planets* pieces, "Jupiter."

"I have the tree," says Robert, dragging it behind him. It's three times as tall as him. "Oh, hi, Harrison! How are you?"

"I'm good," Harrison says, quickly tucking the phone away. "Do you need help with the tree?"

"It's going right behind the ice-cream truck," I say, pointing. I'm a little annoyed; I managed to keep them apart most of the night with setup on opposite sides of the field, but now here they are, and Robert is making big moon eyes at Harrison, and Harrison is smiling back, Clarke almost entirely forgotten. "I didn't realize it was so large. Thank you, Robert, you should go home. Harrison and I can set it up."

"Are you sure?" he asks.

"You look exhausted," I say. "Get some rest. We have a busy weekend."

"All right," he says, staring at Harrison. "See you tomorrow?"

Harrison nods. Oh god, is he blushing?

"Good night," I tell Robert, who waves and walks to the parking lot. I stare at Harrison watching him and then go to pick up one side of the tree. "Come on," I say. Harrison picks up the other end of the tree and we bring it down into the winter scene. I feel a little bad about ruining Robert's chances, but Robert just isn't right for Harrison.

We put the tree down, and after ten minutes of minor adjusting, I think it's perfect. It brings attention to the area and doesn't feel as Christmas-specific as I feared it would. I put my hands on my hips and look around. It really is magical, especially in the thick of it. Besides the twinkle lights, we've made miles of strands of snowflakes, cut from a pearlescent paper, and draped them over all the booths and the entrance. They hang overlapped, creating drapes and thick ropes, shining in different colors as the twinkle lights sparkle on and off next to them. I know it's all excessive, and perhaps I worked the arts and crafts club too hard this year, but only one of them passed out, and the results are magic.

"We should look around once more before turning out the lights, just to double-check," I say.

"You really love this," Harrison says. I start walking, looking at each stall, checking for a light out, a counter askew.

"I love winter carnival," I tell him. "It was the first time I felt really at home at Highbury. Freshman year. It was just...magic."

"Really? What did you do?"

"Oh...well, freshman year I was new. I'd gone to the Jayne School, the small experimental one, you know? Like thirty kids in my grade. And then I was here, surrounded by over a hundred classmates, and truth be told, it was a little overwhelming. I mostly clung to Miles."

"Miles?"

I adjust a snowflake so it covers a scratch in one of the

booths. "Oh yeah, he'd gone to Jayne with me, and we grew up across the street from each other and our moms were best friends.... Miles made friends here faster than I did. I think it was because I'd been the gay kid at Jayne, but here suddenly I was just another new kid, and I had to come out again and it made me feel nervous all over again. Every single person. Plus, Mom had died the year before, which made me... Anyway Miles knew all that, and he was my friend, so we spent the day at the carnival together. He even won me a stuffed rabbit at one of the booths. I think he knew I'd been lonely. He tends to do that, swoop in when he thinks I need rescuing. Condescending jackass."

"Or very kind," Harrison says.

I roll my eyes and adjust the white fabric hanging from one of the booths. "Anyway, he introduced me to a lot of the friends he had made, and when one got a little weird about me, he told him off. And the others backed him up. I think West was one of them, actually. But yeah, I felt like part of the gang. We spent the whole weekend here. Eating Popsicles and playing games and just hanging out. It was... nice."

I look back at the tree. It's perfect. Everything is perfect. "I told him when I was a senior I'd make the carnival our best yet. And I hope I have."

"If you think he's a condescending jackass," Harrison asks, eyes narrowing, "why do you care if you've made it the best?"

"Because otherwise he'd lord it over me," I say.

"I don't know if he would."

"He's different now. He used to be…" I pause, looking for a word that doesn't give away too much. "Sweet."

Harrison's eyes go wide with shock. "You have a crush on him."

Apparently *sweet* was too much. I turn on Harrison, my face stone. "Harrison, if you tell another living soul I swear to god the entire school will know about that ticklish spot on your hip before lunch. And the sound you make when it's touched."

He blushes bright crimson. "Okay, okay, I promise."

"Taylor doesn't even know. We didn't really meet until I went to the Queer Alliance meeting after winter break that year." I swallow. "And besides, I don't have a crush on him. I *had* a crush on him. Past tense and very over. It's normal to have had a crush on the boy next door at some point."

"So not anymore?" Harrison asks as I start walking again, this time to the circuit breaker.

"No. He changed. He used to…it felt like he believed in me, you know? Like he thought I could do anything. I told him I'd make it the best winter carnival ever, and he said, 'I know you will.' Now I think he'd just laugh and say, 'Sure you will' or something." I try doing a haughty laugh, but it's not right. None of this actually sounds like Miles.

"He's hot, though," Harrison says.

"Oh sure. He's very hot," I say. "But he's a condescending jackass."

"I don't know. I'd totally date him."

"Well, you need to raise your standards. And besides, he's straight, so it doesn't apply to either of us. He'll make some girl very unhappy at some point, I'm sure." I open the circuit breaker and turn off the master switch for the area. The winter festival goes dark around us. We start walking to the parking lot.

"Where is he, anyway?" Harrison asks. "He's your VP, he didn't want to be here?"

"His mom got back tonight. She's been gone a year, so I told him he'd better go see her and not even show his face here tonight."

Harrison laughs. "I thought you didn't like him."

"I don't," I say. "But I love his mom."

We're at my car and I open the door. He keeps walking to his.

"See you tomorrow." Harrison waves. I wave back, then get in my car and drive home. Across the street, the lights are on at Miles's place, and I almost want to go visit, to hug Priyanka and smell her vaguely hospital smell, but this is their night. So I'll let them have it. Instead, I go inside, and go up to my room to drop off my bag. And for a moment, I look at the stuffed rabbit on my shelf. Then I roll my eyes and head downstairs to see what health-food horror Dad has made for dinner.

chapter six

FRIDAY I'M EXCUSED FROM MOST OF MY CLASSES SO I CAN MAKE sure everything is ready the moment the winter carnival opens at three, when school gets out. The rest of the student council is out, too, and they help me move in the vendors and clubs, making sure no one ruins the overall aesthetic.

"Taylor, can you help the culinary club with their decor? I appreciate the use of red and green peppers but it's taking away from the overall look."

She nods and takes off.

"Harrison, why don't you help the cheerleaders out, they're having trouble filling the dunk tank."

"I can go, too," Robert says. "The hose is bent, so they might need—"

"No, you need to be at your own booth for the

environmental club. Your giant whale prize is sticking out over the edge of the booth—someone is going to bump into it. Maybe with ice cream."

"Oh!" Robert says, seeing I'm right and running to the booth.

"Okay," Miles says, walking toward me. "The Fair But Frozen Maid truck is perfectly placed, we didn't knock over the tree, and I draped some twinkle lights around the window." He stands next to me, surveying the scene. "It looks really good. I'm impressed you got so much done without me."

"Oh, how could we ever?" I ask, rolling my eyes. "Without your wisdom."

"I just meant I'm sorry I couldn't help. But you did a great job."

I raise my chin slightly, pleased at the compliment. "No need to be sorry. Seeing your mom again is way more important than setup. I know you missed her."

It hangs there a second too long. Missed moms. I blink.

"Well, thanks," he says finally. "And she really wants to see you, too. We were kind of hoping you'd stop by last night, maybe."

"No," I say. "That was your time."

"Well, thanks," he says, and then, strangely, reaches out and squeezes my shoulder with affection. "And really...it's amazing, Emmett. I didn't mean I'm surprised you did it so well without me. I just meant...this is better than even I imagined it. You've outdone your-self, and you already set such a high standard."

I turn to him, my eyebrows arched. "What is with you today? Compliments?"

"I just—" He's smiling wide but stops himself, shaking his head. "I think I'm just really glad my mom is home."

"Well, all right, but this is creeping me out, so please get back to normal Miles ASAP."

"I'm not *that* different," he says, laughing. "Only you would take a compliment and make it so it was somehow an indication that there's something going on with me."

"There he is," I say, satisfied that the old condescend-ing Miles is still in there.

"Uh-huh." He shakes his head. "I'm going to go check that the fried dough booth has a fire extinguisher, just in case." He walks off and I watch everyone put the final touches on their booths. I'm not running any specific booths today, just making sure everything runs smoothly, but I see some of the other council members wandering to their places. I check my watch. Nearly three.

The string quartet shows up—of course I hired them for this—dressed in black, and takes their place to one side of the carnival, on a miked stage. They start playing holiday music, beginning with "Frosty the Snowman." Now it's ready. All that's missing is real snow.

I go to the entrance, a beautiful faux-snowy arch, and the ticket booth, which one of the juniors is running.

Already there's a line of kids from the local middle schools, but she's waiting for me to signal her before I let them in. I look back at everyone else.

"Everyone ready?" I shout.

People shout back variations of yes, so I turn and nod to the ticket-seller. The winter carnival has begun.

The first hour or so is mostly about the smaller kids, but some high schoolers show up and start wandering around, too. No one throws up for the first sixty-two minutes, which I think is a record, but of course some seven-year-old had to have too much fried dough and then get on the Twister. I let one of the freshmen on the student council clean it up.

"Emmett!" I turn around and my father is at the ticket booth. He pays and comes in and gives me a hug. He's in a blue cardigan and jeans, and he's looking around nervously. "This is beautiful, Emmett. I wish there were more flowers, but I guess that's not very snow-themed."

"There are actually snowdrops woven into garlands and wrapped around the fences on every ride," I say, pointing.

"Oh." He smiles and puts his arm around my shoulder, squeezing. "Your mother loved snowdrops." I know, but I don't say anything for a second. "Where's poor Taylor?" he asks. "I want to tell her how the lilac is doing, even if she hasn't come by in a while."

"She's working the health booth," I say, pointing to the booth at the corner. West and Taylor are running it currently, but no one is at the booth, so they're stealing a kiss. As I point, a small child goes running past, knocking into the bowl of condoms they have on the counter. It goes flying and the condoms rain down around the pair of them like flower petals. Condoms now? "This is ridiculous," I mumble.

"What?" Dad asks.

"I said, you should go say hi, but be nice to her boyfriend."

"I will," Dad says, nodding. He's already moving toward them, far away from me. I'll let him go. I have so much to do anyway.

I look at my watch again. The cheerleader dunking booth will be switching out soon. I turn away from the entrance and head toward the environmental club booth, which Harrison has been running. He's selling raffle tickets for the giant stuffed whale.

"Hey, Emmett, you want a raffle ticket?" he asks as I approach.

"Sure," I say, offering him the cash. He takes it and hands me a ticket back.

"Isn't it so cute?" he asks, looking at the giant whale plushie. "I bought like twenty tickets I wanna squish it so bad."

I stare at the whale. It stares back. "Sure. Hey, you have

someone else that can take over? I want you to walk the fair with me, checking to make sure everything is in order."

"Um..." He looks behind him and nods at a sophomore, who nods back. "Okay, I guess." He comes out from behind the booth and follows me as I walk toward the dunking booth. "You don't really need me for this, though, do you? I mean, I like walking with you...but everything is going perfectly, so why—" He stops as Clarke appears, sauntering toward the dunking booth in just a pale pink Speedo. "Oh."

"Hey!" Clarke says, running up to us. "This is so perfect," he says. "The decor, the arrangements, it's the best carnival in years."

"Thank you," I say, beaming. "Harrison helped a lot."

"Ohmigod, you are amazing," Clarke says to Harrison. "The whole council is."

"Um, thanks," Harrison says. He's turned the same shade of pink as Clarke's Speedo.

"Are you blushing because I'm in just my bathing suit?" Clarke asks, grinning wickedly. "You know I dance in it on my KamerUhh videos."

"I know," Harrison says, smiling nervously. "I guess I just didn't expect to see it...in the flesh."

"The flesh?" Clarke grins wickedly. "Wait till you see me get wet. If you can hit the target, I mean," he says, wiggling his eyebrows before walking past us to the dunking booth, hips swaying. It's his turn, and he replaces Alicia on the board above the tub of water, his toes dangling into it.

"C'mon!" Clarke shouts. "Try to get me wet." I can't tell if he's shouting it at Harrison, but it feels like he is.

"Well," I say to Harrison, "you heard the man. Go."

"Oh, I don't know. You have to throw the ball and hit the target and I think I'll just embarrass myself."

"It's from like three feet. Cupid's arrow will guide the ball, I promise," I say, gently shoving him toward the booth. He lines up behind a few others and buys his balls. He misses on the first two, but the third one hits (thank god, failing at this would not be sexy) and with a whoop and a splash, Clarke falls in.

He climbs out of the water and the Speedo clings in ways I find myself staring at before turning away. After all, he's for Harrison. Harrison, who is also staring.

"Sorry," Harrison calls out.

"What for?" Clarke shouts back. "I was getting kind of hot."

Harrison blushes furiously, and I have to lead him away; otherwise, he'll just be staring all day.

"I think he was flirting with me," Harrison says.

"He was totally flirting with you." I pat him on the back. "You're hot, you're funny, people want you. I told you that."

"I guess I didn't believe it. I should probably get back

to the environmental club, though. I'm technically on duty now."

"Sure, I just didn't want you to miss your first opportunity to get Clarke all wet."

"You're terrible," he says. "But thanks. I know I wouldn't even be dreaming of dating Clarke if not for you."

"What are friends for?" I ask. We're at the environmental club booth, but at the entry gate, I can see Miles and his moms. "I better go. I see someone I need to talk to," I say, and pat Harrison on the back before running up to them. Priyanka screams and swoops me into a giant hug. She smells like a hospital, antiseptic with a touch of rose perfume to cover it, and it's weirdly reassuring. I missed her, I realize. I know not as much as Miles did, but I missed her a lot. She was Mom's best friend since they were teenagers, they worked together for years, and seeing her isn't like seeing Mom again, but it's like having a good memory of Mom. A strong one that makes me want to laugh and cry at the same time as I squeeze her tightly. They used to do their sorority cheer together, a chant with some high kicks they'd struggle with, and Priyanka's voice reminds me of that. Of Mom's voice.

"Missed you, Em," she says, letting go. "Miles said this carnival was your baby."

"It was both of us," I say. "All of the council, really. I just..."

"Took control?" Miles offers. He says it almost cutely, which somehow makes it more condescending than usual.

"Only so you had time to see your mom," I tell him.

"I know." He grins, genuinely. "Thanks for that."

"I will also thank you for that, but you should have stopped by, too," Priyanka says. "Jasmine was making that pasta your mom used to love."

"Gnocchi al limone," Jasmine says. "With capers."

"I didn't want to interrupt family time."

"You're family, too, honey." Priyanka wraps her arm around my shoulders. "Now show me this carnival. Miles said there's some special ice-cream truck?"

"Right there," I say, pointing.

"Priyanka!" my dad says from behind us. We turn and she gives Dad a big hug.

"We're getting ice cream," she says to him. "Come on." She offers him her arm, but he looks nervous.

"Ice cream?" Dad says, his voice a little concerned.

"It's the good stuff," Jasmine says.

"I'm a doctor, and I'm insisting on it," Priyanka says. They each link arms on either side of him, *Wizard of Oz* style, and point him at the Fair But Frozen Maid truck. He smiles a little. Miles comes up next to me as we follow them to the truck. He cracks his knuckles, a classic sign of nervousness in him, so I look him up and down, but he just smiles, looking up the ice cream menu on his phone. The line is practically wrapping around the whole festival, so while we wait, Priyanka tells us about her year abroad—scarce medical equipment, disease outbreaks, and food she'd never tried before that she now wants Jasmine to replicate. How it was rewarding, but she missed everyone. She squeezes my arm a lot.

"You look so much like your mom," she says at one point, and I'm quiet, because I don't know what to say to that.

When we get up to the ice-cream truck, we each order—I get the orange hibiscus dark chocolate chip—and then take our cones (or in Dad's case, cup) and wander around the carnival, playing games—I win the balloon race, but Dad beats us all in Skee-Ball. At the dunking booth Miles lands a perfect hit and Alicia falls in a little sideways and the splash bounces off the side of the tank and above the rim, sprinkling water down on Jasmine and Priyanka, who laugh and kiss, looking at each other so in love it feels farcical. This people kissing with things falling on them is becoming a bit much, honestly. And finally, the rides! We start with Dad's penguin ride, a gentle up-and-down loop surrounded by round fluffy penguin statues that flap their wings as you bounce past. Dad laughs with delight the whole time. Then we go on the death drop one together, all getting strapped onto a platform with walls, which suddenly plummets to the earth, then is pulled up again, then down—up and down.

We scream and laugh, and my heart feels like it'll burst out of my mouth with every bounce. Miles looks at me as we plunge back down, his hair flying up, his eyes wide, screaming, and I scream back, and for a moment it feels like old times, when we were best friends, and then we bounce up again and I remember that I don't really like him anymore, and he doesn't really like me, either, but decide to let that go, and remember being friends.

"We should have done ice cream after that," Priyanka says when we get off the ride.

"We can do more ice cream now," I suggest.

"I think one ice cream is enough," Dad says, his voice worried again.

Priyanka puts her hand on Dad's shoulder and squeezes it. "It's just ice cream, Henry," she says. I forgot how she used to do this after Mom died. How she was there to reassure him the way Mom had been.

"Elevated blood sugar can lead to diabetes, which can lead to pancreatic cancer," Dad says. "I read about it."

"In a reputable medical journal?" Priyanka asks. Dad won't meet her eye. I look away, surveying the rest of the festival. "The information isn't exactly wrong, but it's not exactly right, and it's presented in a way meant to excite and scare, so"—I spot Harrison at the environmental club booth, but he's standing in front of it. Robert is behind the counter, pulling a ticket out of a plastic fishbowl, an actual bowl shaped like a fish—"you need to read the actual articles and talk to a doctor. No one here has elevated blood sugar, do they?"

"I don't know, Emmett hasn't let me take his blood in weeks."

I feel Miles's eyes on me. "You okay?" he asks.

"Take his blood?" Priyanka asks.

"Just...," I say. I watch the scene unfold as I hear Priyanka and my dad still talking behind me. Robert draws out a raffle ticket and puts the plastic fishbowl down on the counter, its edge hanging off the side. Starts reading the name. Harrison smiles, then jumps. But then I spot the same small cherubic child who knocked the bowl of condoms running, laughing, smiling, and blissfully unaware of their own physical space, which is about to come into direct contact with the crowd around the raffle. Oh no. I run for them.

"Emmett?" Miles calls. But I leave him behind. Robert is handing Harrison the giant stuffed whale, and Harrison is reaching out to take it, but here comes that child knocking the fishbowl into the air, and all the raffle tickets go flying up, about to rain down—

"Wait," I say, pulling Harrison back. I got there in time. The raffle tickets fall to the ground, around Robert alone, just making a mess. I've seen enough of things falling down around people lately that I know what it does to them, and Robert and Harrison should not be the ones to experience that. *Clarke* and Harrison should be.

"What?" Harrison says, confused. He turns and looks at me. "Emmett?"

"Sorry," I say, realizing I have to make up an excuse. "I thought I saw a kid with ice cream about to run into the whale, but he swerved."

"Oh." Harrison laughs, then turns back to Robert and takes the whale and gives it a big hug. "I won! Isn't it so cute!"

"It is," I say. "You should go show Clarke. He just finished his second shift at the dunking booth."

"Oh yeah," he says, hugging the whale tightly, his eyes wide. "Maybe he can help me name him."

"That's a great idea," I say, genuinely impressed.

"Emmett!" I turn around. Jasmine is waving for me to come back.

"I gotta go," I say. "Have fun."

I walk back to Jasmine, Miles, Priyanka, and Dad.

"Who was that?" Jasmine asks. "Boyfriend?"

"Emmett doesn't date!" Dad says quickly, maybe too loudly, as a few people stop and stare. "He knows better than that."

"It's fine if he dates and uses protection, Henry," Jasmine says, reaching out and squeezing Dad's hand. "If he's even having sex."

"He's just a friend," I say, my face feeling hot. "I'm setting him up with someone else, in fact. Let's go see the ring toss!" I point and thankfully they all start walking, ice cream, syringes, and sex lives forgotten. But Miles hangs back with me as we walk.

"You pulled him away pretty quick," Miles says. "Worried about something?"

"You've seen how romantic it's been around here. Things falling on people in artistic romance-novel-cover ways. It's ridiculous is what it is. Something in the weather maybe."

"The weather?"

"Well, what else could it be?" I ask, gesturing in front of me in exasperation. He shrugs. I take a breath. "In any case, I didn't want anyone getting confused by a moment with raffle tickets raining down, pretty and..."

"Romantic?" Miles asks. "You wanted to stop a romantic moment?"

I put my hands on my hips, trying to find words. "An incorrect romantic moment," I say.

Miles laughs. He's so insufferable. "You're so keen to get everything right," he says, shaking his head. "Sometimes you have to just let stuff happen."

"I've already told you: Life is messy. I keep it neat. Otherwise—"

"Yes, I know, I know, lovers, friends, romance, all from the same pot, and you don't want to get your heart broken by falling in love before twenty-five."

"You make it sound so trivial—it's not about not wanting my heart broken. It's about avoiding pain because—"

I glance at my dad, who's eyeing the sex education booth again, looking suspicious.

"Emmett," Miles says. "Come on, that's not the same."

"What's not?" I ask.

He looks at me in silence and I stare back, my chin raised a little.

"Hey, guys!" We're at the ring toss, and of course Georgia is running it. This was supposed to be my solace. I should have memorized her schedule to make sure this didn't happen. She's standing behind the counter in front of all the pegs on a board you need to toss a small ring onto. Above her, hanging like curtains, are strings of small stuffed animals, including several of our school mascot, Helena the Highbury Hippo, who wears the full blue-and-yellow uniform (pants, not skirt) and a big matching bow around her neck in lieu of a tie.

"Hey, Georgia. These are my moms and Emmett's dad," Miles says.

"How's it going so far?" I ask.

"We're really raking it in," she says. "Your idea to have gift cards as prizes has attracted a much older crowd than last year. I mean the little ones still play for these stuffed toys, but teenagers and adults are playing for the gift cards."

I smile. I was proud of that idea. "Excellent," I say. "But I will be playing for one of the Helenas, as I want to take one with me next year to Stanford."

"All right," she says. "Five bucks for five rings. You

need to get all five for a big Helena, but only three for a small one."

Jasmine claps her hands. "You got this, Emmett," she says.

"Sophomore year, John got five in a row," Georgia adds. I try not to scowl, and throw the first ring. It wraps soundly around the mouth of a bottle, hula-hooping for a moment before falling.

"YES!" Jasmine shouts. I smile. It wasn't the bottle I was aiming for, but no one needs to know that. I toss another, and it goes exactly where I want, wrapping around another bottle. Jasmine claps. The third bounces off the bottle I was aiming for but then falls around the one next to it.

"That's three!" Georgia says. "You can have one of the small Helenas. But if you get the next two you get a big one! And I get to tell John someone tied him."

I smile and shake my head. "A little one is all I need, thank you."

"Oh come on," Miles says. "You have two rings left. Better to just use them, right?"

"Go for it!" Jasmine shouts.

"Honey, it's just a game," Priyanka says.

"If I have what I need, I don't need to try for more and lose," I say. "Especially not if it means Georgia is going to make it into a whole John comparison," I add in a whisper to Miles.

"Can I use them, then?" Miles asks. "If I get the last two, it's still five rings, right?"

"Um...I guess so?" Georgia shrugs. "I mean, technically you two are in charge, so...you can just take one."

"No, we can't," I say. "And I don't know about the rings, either. Shouldn't it all be—"

But before I can finish my sentence, Miles has picked up a ring, tossed it in the air, and caught it, showing off, and then looped it around a bottle in the front row.

"Four," he says, taking the final ring. "Last one. If I get this, you get to bring one of those big Helenas to your dorm room."

"All right," I say, rolling my eyes. "As long as this isn't just a ploy so you can go around telling people you won me a giant Helena."

"Oh," Miles says, tossing the ring up and catching it again, "that's exactly what it is."

He tosses the final ring, and it hits the side bottle, bounces high, and then impossibly lands directly over the mouth of the centermost bottle.

"YESSSSS!!!!!" Jasmine shouts, jumping up in the air.

"Way too into this," Priyanka says.

"That ring could have bounced off the bottle and taken someone's eye out," Dad says.

I sigh as Georgia gets down one of the larger Helenas. She looks back and forth between me and Miles. "I don't know who to give this to."

"Here," Miles says, taking it and then handing it to me. "Look what I won you!"

"I got three of those rings," I say. "I won this more than you did."

"Fine." Miles laughs. "You won it."

"You helped," I concede, taking the Helena. "Thank you. She'll look excellent in my dorm room."

"You have a whole plan for the room already?" he asks.

"No, no," Dad interrupts. "I've been terrible—we haven't gone shopping at all. I want to get him a mini-fridge big enough for a large pitcher, one of the ones you just leave the green tea in overnight to diffuse. Probably two of them. And we need to find the perfect first aid kit."

I make myself smile. "We will, Dad. I know we'll find the perfect one."

"Oh, anything can be a first aid kit," Priyanka says. "We use one of my grandma's old sewing boxes."

"No, no, no," Dad says. "Top of the line only."

"We'll find one," I say quickly, before this becomes a real conversation. "I should go put this away in my car. I don't want to get ice cream on it or anything." I hold up my Helena. "You'll all be okay on your own?" I ask, looking at Dad.

"We'll be fine," Priyanka says.

"Great," I say, "I'll find you in a bit." I turn away quickly. I can feel my eyes stinging a little, my face warm, and I'm not sure why.

"Hey, wait," Miles says, jogging next to me. "You okay?"

"Sure." I smile.

"Your dad seems…"

"It's the usual," I say, "don't worry. Go hang out with your moms."

I walk faster, and Miles turns around and goes back to the parents. I know this is all because I'm leaving. Dad'll be alone, and that scares him. It scares me, too.

"Hey, you win that?" I glance up. I'm walking by the dunking booth, and Clarke is standing outside it, dripping wet in just his Speedo. Harrison next to him, smiling a little too largely.

"I did!" I say, smiling. "I wanted one for my dorm. Miles technically helped, but I won it."

"Technically?" Harrison asks.

"Did Georgia bring out her John score chart?" Clarke asks.

I laugh. "She did."

Harrison frowns. "What?"

"She just always feels a need to compare everything happening to how John would do it, or how John did it, or what John is doing now," Clarke says, waving his hand in her general direction. "It's full stalker behavior."

I laugh again.

"I think she just misses him," Harrison says. "They're best friends."

Clarke shrugs. "Sure, yeah. That makes it sad, I guess."

"Or kind of sweet," Harrison says, looking at me.

"Cloyingly," I say. Clarke laughs. "I'm going to go put this in my car before someone gets it wet," I add, holding it far away from Clarke. "You two better stop by Fair But Frozen Maid before they run out of the good flavors."

"Oh yeah. We'll see you there?" Clarke asks.

"I already had some. The orange hibiscus dark chocolate chip is fantastic."

"I'll have to try it," Clarke says. "Post a review on KamerUhh."

"You should," I say. "Be sure to mention the carnival."

"Oh, I already posted a bunch of me in my Speedo talking about it."

"A bunch of guys from other schools came just to dunk him," Harrison says.

"Good work," I say. "Go get ice cream."

"Later, Emmett," Clarke says, waving.

"Later!" Harrison says. I walk away and get to my car, where I put Helena in the passenger seat and belt her in place, for safety. When I lock the car and turn back to the carnival, I take a deep, sudden breath. The sky is darker now, rose and tangerine, and the lights are twinkling so vibrantly, it looks beautiful. People are laughing and I hear kids on rides, and it just looks so perfect.

I know I should go back to the fair. I need to oversee everything, and I should make sure Dad isn't being too much of a handful. But for a moment, I just want to watch, and I do. Mom would really like this, I think. I take a breath. Vanilla and pine. I wonder if that's what snow smells like.

Then it's back into the carnival. I say hi to Dad and Miles and his moms, but then another kid vomits and everyone else is busy, so I go clean it up. And then the health booth runs out of condoms after a bunch of freshman boys each take a handful. Fair But Frozen Maid runs out of ice cream, and as the sun sets, most of the kids drift out, until it's just teenagers, going on mostly empty rides. We close at nine, and I go around gathering up all the money from the rides and entry tickets and putting it in the lockbox. Over ten grand, just in one day. That more than pays our costs and gives us a nice amount to donate afterward, too. The school takes 30 percent of our profits, and it's customary for the student council to raise that to 50 percent, but the other half goes to a charity of the board's choosing. With so many causes, it wasn't easy, but I managed to convince everyone that this year it should go to the National Cervical Cancer Coalition. It's not in honor of Mom, officially, but in my mind it is.

After we shoo out the last of the teenagers, I gather everyone together at the entrance to thank them for their hard work. Dad and Miles's moms wait outside, watching us. Normally one of the coheads of the student council gives a speech now, so I turn to Miles, but he just shakes his head.

"You did this," he says, and spreads out his hand to let me step forward.

I smile and do so. "Thank you, everyone," I say to the council and volunteers. "We have had one of the best opening nights in winter carnival history. We've made over ten thousand dollars, and that was just tonight. With tomorrow and Sunday, I fully expect us to cross fifty thousand dollars in profit, which means twenty-five thousand dollars for the school, enough for those new memory foam seats in the theater! Finally, the only discomfort we'll feel watching the spring musical will be from the performances." Miles elbows me. "Kidding, kidding! Our musicals are always top-notch. And with a little luck and work, our seating will match them. And, on top of that, we'll have so much money to give to the NCCC, which is just..." I take a breath, and Miles puts his hand on my shoulder, which is enough to stop any flood of emotions that might have threatened and replace them with a vague annoyance that he felt I needed reassurance. I square my shoulders, and he removes his hand.

"Thank you," I say. "Excellent work today, everybody, and keep it up for the next few days. The work schedule is in all your inboxes, but we have a paper copy inside the ticket booth if your phone dies. See you all tomorrow!"

I wave at everyone as they leave, and then lock up the gates that lead to the fairground and turn off the power.

"I didn't know you were raising money for the NCCC," Dad says as we walk back to our cars. "I can match any donation, you know, double it."

"If you want," I say. "But separately, please. I want this to be something we did."

"*You* did, really," Miles says.

"No. This isn't like Helena. You didn't just help. We all did this together," I say.

"Well, I thought it was fantastic," Priyanka says. "Felt like a welcome-back party just for me."

"Should we all go somewhere and get dinner?" Jasmine asks. "Casa Verde probably has a table for us."

"They always have a table for you, Mom," Miles says. "But...I think I'd just like to go home. That's okay, right?"

"Sure, honey," Jasmine says. "You've had a long day. I can cook. Emmett, Henry, you want to come over?"

I glance over at Miles. He looks a little nervous, suddenly, and won't meet my eyes.

"That's kind of you," I say. "But I think we'll just head home."

"What?" Dad says.

"I still have to study for midterms," I say. "I was just going to eat while reading."

"That makes sense," Priyanka says, though she

frowns a little. "Well, after the fair and midterms are over then. Family dinner at our place."

"That sounds great," I say with a smile.

"Yeah," Miles says. He cracks one of his knuckles. He did that earlier, too, but I'm not sure what he could be nervous about.

We drop Miles's moms off at their car, and then my dad at his. Thank god the cars are all electric, or this would be terrible for the environment. Then Miles and I keep walking to the student parking lot. It's dark and everyone else is gone, so the world feels empty.

"You all right?" I ask him. I don't know why, exactly. We've had a nice day together, and it feels a little like old times, maybe.

"Huh?" He looks up at me, then smiles. "I've always been so obvious to you."

"You're obvious to everyone. So what is it?"

"Oh, it's just…I need to talk to my moms about something, and I told myself I'd do it tonight, and now I'm nervous."

"What, is there a chance you'll only get a B-plus in statistics?"

He scowls, then laughs. "Yes, that's it."

"I'm sure they'll forgive you," I say as we arrive at my car. I open the door. He looks curiously at Helena, strapped in and sitting shotgun. "For her protection," I say.

He laughs again. "Night, Emmett. See you tomorrow."

"You too," I say, and get in and close the door. I watch him walk over to his car, then pull out of the parking lot. Today went well, but it was exhausting, too. Still, so much is on track: the festival, Harrison and Clarke, and I have a Helena ready for my dorm room. Everything is going exactly like I planned it. A perfect day.

chapter seven

THE REST OF THE WEEKEND IS SO BUSY I BARELY HAVE TIME TO THINK about anything besides the festival. Friday it was only half a day, but Saturday is from morning until night, and I'm on-site the entire time, cleaning puke, restocking condoms, running the ring toss booth, the health booth, the balloon pop booth. At one point the power goes out to the Fair But Frozen Maid truck and I need to stop the whole festival so I can flip a breaker. Sunday is almost the same, except some money goes missing until it turns up in a cashbox a freshman forgot to bring to me. And then we have strike, take down all the decorations, unwind the twinkling lights, pack away the giant fake tree again. By Sunday night, my muscles are so sore I feel like I can't move, and all I want to do is sleep for a week. So it's perfect timing for midterms.

With all the distraction, I'm not even annoyed that

Clarke and Harrison haven't gone on an official date yet. If I were Clarke, I'd be waiting until after midterms anyway. Sure, that first day at the festival would have been perfect, they could have gone for another ice cream, but knowing Clarke, another ice cream wasn't on the menu if he was going to be in a Speedo every day. And honestly, I'd feel the same. But clearly sparks were flying, so I decide to leave it until after midterms. If they don't have a date by Friday, then perhaps my intervention will be required again. It's really a bit much, at this point. But like the festival, sometimes nothing would get done without me.

So I study and get ready for tests, and the student council has a little ceremony and photo shoot of us with the seats in the theater to show what we've accomplished (the email we send to the student body is all photos of us in the theater chairs and the slogan "Remember when you sit, we all earned it" to give everyone a sense of accomplishment). The NCCC money I write as a check, from the school checkbook, and mail in, after calling ahead. They say thank you and promise to send someone to the school to talk about cervical cancer, if we ever want them to. Dad would love that, but the principal says our health classes cover it, so I don't mention it to him.

Dad's very proud when I tell him how much we raised. He tears up so much he becomes worried about allergies and makes us both eat a tangerine for the vitamin C to help bolster our immune systems.

And then there are midterms. I think I'll do all right with them. I've been studying, and I've never been bad at tests. It would be awful to lose my ranking this late in my high school career, but I can't see myself dropping much. Certainly not enough to worry about Stanford rescinding their acceptance.

By the end of the week, I still feel like I need to go lie down, but at least now I can for a weekend. Well, not the whole weekend. There's still Taylor's party on Saturday.

"You'll come over today after school to help me prep, right?" she asks on Friday as we leave our AP History midterm.

"Prep what?" I ask. "You don't need to decorate."

"Well, first of all yes, I do, but also I just want to make sure we have enough"—she leans in, whispering— "alcohol."

"Taylor, you've drunk before, this isn't a secret."

"I know, but I basically just have beer. I don't know those fancy mixed drinks. Come over, look at my parents' collection, tell me what we need. Andre can bring anything we don't have."

"I thought he was just a sophomore," I say. "And studying abroad this semester."

"Well, he'll be back for the party, obviously," Taylor says, brushing her hair behind her ear. "It's so you two can meet."

"No, it's not."

"And he has a fake ID. He's had it for years, apparently."

"So he's an alcoholic?" I ask as we arrive at our lockers. I open mine and put away my history textbooks, and take out my math.

"No," she says, frowning. "I just mean…look, come over tonight, okay? I've never thrown a party before and I don't know what I'm doing. I'm an art nerd. You're the cool one."

"I am, aren't I?" I say, smiling.

"Shut up," she says, but she's grinning, too. "You coming to the cafeteria for lunch?"

"Yes, but I must study, can't talk."

"Same, let's cram together."

So we go to the cafeteria, where I eat blueberries one by one as I drink my iced green tea and go over my notes for statistics. Statistics are very important in medicine. The string quartet plays softly below the quiet murmurs of conversation. It's a wonderful way to study.

The midterm goes well enough, with me only being a little slipped up by a graph with irregular time intervals (a cheap trick from Ms. Schneider, but not surprising considering the outrageous heels she always wears to class), and then I'm done. Free! Which means I can once again focus on more important matters.

I spot Clarke in the hallway. He's in his full cheerleader uniform, the shorts very short and tight, and wearing a pale blue headband. He smiles when he sees me.

"We have a little postmidterm practice party," he says to me. "I can see you judging me for wearing my uniform in the halls."

"I would never." I lean on the locker next to his.

"Oh right, you're too nice. I mean, you can join if you want. Alicia has a fake ID, so we basically just drink vodka tonics and try to do flips. It's pretty chill."

"Oh," I say, a little confused. He's probably just being polite. "Thanks, but I promised I'd help Taylor prep for her party tomorrow."

"No worries." He shrugs, then bends down to pick up his backpack. It's a nice bend. Harrison is going to be very lucky. Clarke stands back up and smiles at me. "I know we've been kind of dodging around it, who's going to ask who out first, but fine, I'll give in."

"You will?" I ask. "Good, because I don't think—"

"So that's a yes?" He smiles wickedly.

I'm confused. "What? I mean, I'm sure Harrison will say yes, but you have to go ask him out, I'm not going to be messenger."

"Harrison?" He raises an eyebrow. "No, you, Emmett. I'm asking you out. Finally."

"No." I shake my head. "No, you're supposed to ask Harrison out. I don't date, Clarke. You know that. Everyone knows that."

He frowns, puts his hands on his hips. "Wait, so inviting me to the group hang, the flirting at the carnival...

I thought you were saying maybe your stupid little rule could be broken for me."

"I wasn't flirting."

"You were definitely checking me out."

"No," I say. This is going all wrong. I feel my body getting warm, feverish. That can't be good. "Listen. I was trying to set you up with Harrison."

Clarke laughs, and I keep staring at him. He stops. "Oh. You're serious."

"Yeah."

"So you're saying no to going out with me?" He looks like I just slapped him.

"I want you to go out with Harrison," I say, maybe a little louder than I should. I look around, but no one is paying attention.

"I'm not going out with Harrison." He rolls his eyes. "As if."

"Why not?"

"He has like no followers on KamerUhh. You have ten thousand. Not bad, enough to work with. I'm almost at fifty, but I need new content. Couple content. It would be so good, Emmett: you, me, black-and-white photos of us cuddling on the beach with only a heart emoji as the caption, us in matching onesie pajamas around a Christmas tree for the holidays, videos of us alluding to, or just outright saying, who the top and bottom are. People love that stuff from gay couples. We could get sponsorships!

And from there the world would be ours—you want to be a doctor, right? Doctors who are famous on social media can get so much information out to people. I'd have my choice of cheer teams. And you're so perfect for it. Social media is how we can make our futures."

I feel the breath go out of me. "So make your future with Harrison," I say, my voice raspy. "You made him your lock screen!" It sounds like I'm begging.

"I made *us* my lock screen," he says, pulling out his phone and showing it to me. It's the photo of the three of us, but Harrison has been cut out, so it's just Clarke, me, and a random hand. It feels like my whole body is cramping.

"But Harrison—"

"No. He's not perfect for what I need, or what I want. You are. And don't pretend like you don't want it. I'm not saying we have to be exclusive or anything—we can be very chill. But we'd look cute together, and speaking frankly, I'm amazing in bed. I'm guessing you are, too." He steps forward.

"Clarke...Harrison is totally into you. I've been telling him for weeks that you two should be an item. He's my friend, I could never. And I don't want to. I thought you and me were just friends."

He sighs and steps back. "We can't be just friends, Emmett. That would be way too messy." He looks me up and down, his mouth pinched. "Your loss." He walks away, his hips swaying as he does. I have been staring, he's right. Somewhere, the string quartet, maybe happy to be done with midterms, starts playing again, starting with Taylor Swift's "Anti-Hero."

What am I going to tell Harrison? And how could I have misread this? I still feel feverish, and shaky now, too. I should have let Dad run a blood test this week. Could I have something? I swallow and take a deep breath. No. This is just…embarrassment. Shame. Because I messed this up and now Harrison is going to get hurt because of it. I feel my eyes fleck with tears and head out to the parking lot, where the air is cool. There are speakers out here, too, but they've moved on to Tchaikovsky's Sixth. Which is fine, it suits my mood. I take another breath, but now my nose is running, which never happens. I go to my car, quickly, and lean in to search the glove compartment for tissues, and manage to find a pink packet of them, with just one left. It smells like plastic, but I blow my nose into it anyway.

"Hey," a voice says behind me. I turn around. Harrison. I feel like I'm dying.

"Hi," I say, my voice wavering.

He narrows his eyes. "You okay?"

I should tell him. I *need* to tell him. But this information, this terrible misunderstanding I've created, it's like a disease, and if it's hurting me this badly, it will kill him. It can wait. Maybe I can find someone else for him first. Maybe I can—

"Emmett? You okay?"

I shake my head, force a smile. Breaking his heart wouldn't be nice. "Just going over my last midterms. Statistics. I think I might have messed up the final problem."

"I'm sure you did fine," he says. He's so nice. He deserves better than Clarke anyway. To be more than just a prop for likes. "So, I was thinking about asking Clarke to go to Taylor's party tomorrow, like...as a date. Is that a good idea?"

I swallow. "Oh, well...we just finished midterms and I think he's doing that cheerleader party thing tonight, so...maybe ask him at the party?" No, that's bad, too, I realize, the moment it's out of my mouth.

"Oh." He tilts his head. "Yeah, that makes sense. Thanks, Emmett." He smiles, a little shy. "I admit this whole you setting me up thing was kind of weird at first, but I feel like I can do it now. I can ask out a hot guy I thought was out of my league. So thank you for that."

My body cramps again. I smile. "You're welcome." I need to tell him.

"See you at the party tomorrow," he says, walking away.

"Yeah, and Harrison..." He turns around, happy, grinning. "Just. You're great. You deserve the best relationship. So it's not me that's done this. It's you."

He beams. Glows. Is genuinely thrilled. "You don't have to say that."

"I mean it. You're great. You deserve the best."

He's blushing now. "I feel like you're hitting on me now," he says. "So I'm going to walk away before I get confused."

I laugh. "Okay. See you tomorrow."

I'll tell him tomorrow, I decide, watching him walk away. He doesn't move his hips the way Clarke does, but there's something sexy in him, too, and I wasn't lying. He deserves the best. I thought that was Clarke, but I guess I fucked that up and now... I sigh and sit down in my car, on the passenger side, the door still open. How do I fix this? Who else would be a good match for Harrison that I can get to ask him out before he asks Clarke out? That's the best fix, I think.

"Hey." I look up. It's Taylor. "Don't forget you're coming over to—" Her eyebrows furrow. "What's wrong?"

I smile. "What?"

"Emmett." She taps her foot.

"I..." She can always see through me. It makes me feel like crying. "Let's talk about it at your place."

"Okay. Then I'm driving. West picked me up today anyway."

She goes around and gets behind the wheel of my car and I hand her my keys as I close the door.

"I messed up," I say, and suddenly I'm crying, and it feels like a relief.

By the time we get to her place, I've explained it. Clarke liking me, like an asshole.

She sighs as she parks the car, then turns to me.

"Okay. I get what's happening. You feel like you failed. You never fail. You're Emmett. So this is shocking and awful for you, and it sucks, and I am a hundred percent here for you. But maybe you need to stay out of it. Maybe it's not your job to find Harrison a boyfriend. I know you want to be nice, but maybe that's *too* nice."

"But he's my friend. And I found you a boyfriend!"

"Well...what happened was you saw us making eyes at each other and said to West, 'Oh, would you just ask her out already,' and he did."

"Exactly," I say, getting out of the car. "I saw the spark, and I made it happen."

"Well, look," she says, getting out behind me and leading me in through the garage, "I'm not saying I'm not grateful and that maybe we needed that push, but it was already pretty obvious we liked each other. You didn't try to *make* us like each other."

I nod. She's right. Just because I had such good intuition with my first round of matchmaking doesn't mean the second was going to be easier.

"I mean, they had a spark," I say as we walk into her house and head to the kitchen. Her parents don't have much style, but the kitchen is clean and white and big windows let in a lot of light. "I just didn't realize that Clarke was looking for likes more than love. I think you're right. My intuition is good, but that doesn't mean that the people I'm setting up can see it."

"That's not quite—"

"I need to find someone for Harrison who he has real chemistry with. I can't just prepare a man for him—preparation is the problem. It ruins happiness, foolish preparation. So tomorrow, at the party, I'll just see who he has chemistry with and take it from there. Someone he clicks with. Or at least someone who I think isn't superficial. Someone who really sees him."

"I mean that's a good idea, sure…" She trails off. "Let's just look at what's in the liquor cabinet, okay?"

"Yes," I say. "Thank you. I feel much better about this now." And I do. "Thank you so much for being such a good friend. I hate when I lose sight of…who I am. But you always remind me."

She turns and light from the window catches her, and she smiles, a little shy. "Shut up," she says. "How much vodka do you think we need?"

We talk about alcohol and mixers while decorating a little, and then order Chinese. Her parents are out of town, and West is having dinner with his family because his brother just got in. Afterward, we put on a bad movie and try each of the alcohols in the cabinet to see which are worth getting more of.

The house is this big Bel Air–style mansion, perfect for a party, but the truth is, I have no idea where Taylor got her artistic eye from. Her parents' decorating taste is, and I'm not trying to be rude, bland. White walls in the foyer, beige walls in the living room, white again in the sunroom. The only art they have is family pictures, which is sweet, I suppose, but they're all small things, framed and circling each room in the sort of pattern that looks like a computer came up with it. It's all very tidy, but it's not very interesting. Taylor's room is gorgeous, though, with zebra sheets and pale pink walls. So even with the living room available, we hang out up there and make sure we have a sense of the guest list.

"We need to make sure all the gays are there," I tell her. "So there are options for Harrison. Someone sincere, and kind."

"You know, I think Robert has a crush on him."

I wave her off. "I barely remember Robert when he's in the room with me," I say. "We can do better."

"But isn't it about if Harrison notices him? Chemistry, like you said?"

I think about it a moment. She's right, so I nod. "All right, you can invite him, but I still think we can do better."

"He," she says, pulling out her phone.

"What?"

"Not 'we can do better.' He can do better."

"Did I say *we*? Slip of the tongue."

She messages Robert on KamerUhh (he has an account mostly about endangered animals) to let him know about the party.

"I'm more excited about the one boy I'm bringing for you," she says, nudging me with her shoulder.

I laugh. "Still? Taylor, I told you, we'll be family forever, even if we don't marry brothers before we're twenty."

"I know," she says. "But like...don't you want a boyfriend? Don't you want to kiss in the rain?"

"I'd want to kiss in the snow," I say, letting myself think about it for a moment—his lips closing in on mine, cold snowflakes dotting his dark eyelashes, the chilly flecks making me shiver as his warm arms wrap around me...I shake my head. "But it would end poorly. You know my feelings on this."

"Emmett..." She opens her mouth, then closes it, turns back to the movie, then shakes her head and turns back to me. "Emmett, I get why you'd feel like maybe a relationship ending is bad. Especially you. But having one is still—"

"What do you mean especially me?" I ask. I shiver.

"I mean..." She takes a deep breath. "You've had a relationship end in the worst way. But breaking up with someone isn't the same as your mom dying. And besides, maybe your brain isn't fully developed until you're twenty-five or whatever, but that doesn't mean anything. You and someone you love can develop into people who still love each other."

"That seems very unlikely to happen. And it has nothing to do with my mother." I turn back to the movie. I don't want to talk about this. Yes, obviously, losing my mother was painful. Is still painful. Worse than that. It's like part of me is missing. And yes, I've wondered if maybe that means I have to grow it back before I can fall in love, if it'll ever grow back at all... but that's not why I don't want a boyfriend. "It's complicated," I say after she doesn't say anything for a while. "It's messy. I don't like messy, you know that. Boyfriends, friends, sex... you have to put up barriers, figure out who's who, otherwise it's just drama. Think of your jewelry. Each piece has to be a ring or a necklace or an earring. You can't just switch them around. And in high school, having to see the person every day... it's cleaner this way."

"Is it?" She raises an eyebrow.

"It is." I nod, definitively.

"So trying to find a boyfriend for the guy you've been having sex with isn't messy?"

The room goes silent. I turn slowly to look at her, my skin feeling hot. "How long have you known?"

"Since it started." She lifts an eyebrow. "Harrison doesn't need a tutor."

I frown, ready for her to yell at me about secrets.

"I'm not angry," she says first. "Your sex life is your business, and if you just want to be friends with benefits, that's fine... but, Emmett. You can put a ring on a chain and it becomes a necklace. Relationships aren't just cut-and-dry labels. Especially not for queer people. It's going to be messy. And messy can hurt, but sometimes it's great, too."

"I prefer it when things are tidy, and they can be," I say.

"Only if everyone agrees. Like back when we first met, when I hadn't realized I was trans yet, and we thought we were two gay guys. Why didn't we ever hook up?"

"I don't know. We never had that vibe, did we? You said I was your first other gay friend, and you were mine and…"

"And after a month of hanging out all the time, I said to you, 'I want you to be my friend forever, and nothing should get in the way of that,' and you agreed. We put up lines. Defined ourselves. Have you done that with Harrison?"

"I thought so. He's the one who approached me, you know. I didn't seduce a junior into something sordid. He said we should spend time together, and he meant naked, and we did."

"And you never thought he might also wonder where it could go? Sometimes romance, especially for us queers, can start physical and then become friendship and then romance."

"I've always been clear I don't want a boyfriend, haven't I?"

"Look, I think you were probably pretty clear at first. But I think sometimes you're just so, well, nice"—she laughs—"that people can see what they want. I did, once. That's why I told you that we would only be friends. I thought I was dumping you."

I feel my eyebrows rise. "What?"

"I thought you had a thing for me. And we weren't

even sleeping together. It's that thing, you know, when your friends and lovers all come from the same pool...."

I nod. "I know."

"Sometimes maybe because of that, lines are fuzzier than we think...and it can get messy. And maybe you being nice to Harrison and sleeping with him, and then all this matchmaking, is confusing to him...and to you. Did you just volunteer to do it because he was catching feelings? I mean he must have told you he wanted a boyfriend. And you were already someone he was..."

I tilt my head away from her. "Maybe it was a little, at first...but I want him to be happy, genuinely. I care about him."

"I mean...you'd be a cute couple. If you care about him, want him to be happy, and like having sex with him—why not?"

I sit back down and sigh. "I don't know. I just think..." I look at my arm. There's still a faint bruise from when Dad took my blood last weekend. I let him because I wanted to make sure I was in tip-top shape going into midterms. The bruise is a faded blue and green, small. I don't think anyone else would even notice it, but to me it looks sad. "I just don't want a breakup. I don't want that. So I don't want a boyfriend. He does. This is the easiest solution."

"Okay," she says. "Well...I hope you like Andre anyway. I've maaaaybe talked you up to him a little too much."

"How? You haven't even met him."

"When West FaceTimes him. We talk. He's really nice; you'll like him. He's funny—witty, really—like you. And cute."

"I mean, if you don't have a problem with me just using him for sex, with Harrison looking for a boyfriend, I could use a new—"

She shoves me. "Absolutely not. You gotta date him or nothing. Otherwise it's messy for *me*."

I sigh. "Well, we'll see if I like him."

"You will. And you should...let yourself be open to it. It's not like you'd have much time to date him and break up before he goes back to college. Maybe it could be like a weeklong affair and ends with a bittersweet but inevitable parting, and then you reunite at Stanford. That would be romantic, wouldn't it?"

"Maybe," I say, imagining it.

"Yeah, yeah." She rolls her eyes. "You can't fool me, Emmett. Just because you don't want a breakup doesn't mean you don't want a boyfriend."

I look at the movie. She's not wrong.

"Just think," she says, leaning into me, "you could kiss him in the snow...."

"I wouldn't mind that," I say, so softly I don't think she hears me. "It might be nice."

chapter eight

I SLEEP IN ON SATURDAY, BECAUSE I FINALLY CAN. I MAKE MYSELF eggs while Dad does an hour on his treadmill watching some gardening show. Today I am just going to enjoy myself. And fix the Harrison thing. Find him a new man. I've been going over the list again in my head, making sure key people were invited to Taylor's party, but the truth is, none of them seem quite right. Maybe Jimmy broke up with his boyfriend, there was a rumor like that. And if we could get Ethan to at least use some cologne so the pot smell isn't so overpowering... No, no, I'm doing what I did last time. I need to see them all in action. See chemistry, like Taylor said. The same way I matched her with West.

But first I need to tell Harrison it's not happening with Clarke. I'll do that tonight. First thing at the party, tear off the Band-Aid, so we can focus on finding him someone else.

Miles texts me to see if I want to go to the party together tonight. He volunteers to drive home so I can drink. I text him back that I will accept his generous offer, which he responds to with the laugh-crying emoji, for some reason. The rest of the day I spend going over the men some more in my head. Even though I know it's not the right way to do it, I can't seem to stop. So I shower, snack on some grapes, eat a quick dinner of a sandwich, and put on an excellent outfit—a very well-fitted royal-blue sweater and some gray jeans. Then I go across the street to meet Miles. He's waiting for me, look-ing…odd. Lighter? Happier?

"What's wrong with you?" I ask, approaching.

He laughs. "Nothing. What? I'm great."

"Yes, I can tell."

He laughs again. "So you think me being happy is bad?"

"No," I say quickly. "I just mean…I thought maybe you were faking it for some reason, overcompensating."

He rolls his eyes and hands me the keys to his car. "I'm great. You drive there, I'll drive back?"

"Sure," I say.

He cracks his knuckles, nervous.

"Are you sure you're all right?" I say, getting behind the wheel.

"I really am."

"Well, good," I say, pulling out of the driveway. "Me too. Clarke isn't interested in Harrison, but I'm going to fix it. I know what I did wrong."

"Oh? Well, that's great. I actually—"

"Yes. The problem is, I didn't really look for chemistry before. That's why I set up Taylor and West. They were so clearly into each other. And that's what I need to look for."

"I think you're right. I think—"

"But the problem is, I don't know who that could be. And I need to tell Harrison about Clarke first."

"Oh, that's—"

"Going to be difficult, yes."

Miles starts laughing suddenly. And he keeps laughing enough that I turn to him at the stop sign, glaring.

"You think his heartbreak is funny?"

"No," he says, still laughing, quickly shaking his head. "Sorry, no." He stops laughing. "I was just laughing because I couldn't get a word in edgewise."

"Oh," I say. He's right. "Sorry. Did you have something you wanted to tell me?"

He suddenly goes still. Palpably silent. Then he shakes his head. "Just...why is this so important to you? Finding a boyfriend for Harrison. I assume things between the two of you are over, right?"

"Yes, obviously. But he's still my friend. So I want him to be happy. I know a boyfriend isn't for me...no."

I shake my head. "I talked about it with Taylor, and I should be more honest with myself. It's the breakup I don't want. The pain of that. But my friends, like Harrison and Taylor, people I care about, they're less fragile than I am. They're willing to risk it. They're sturdy enough for love. And I want them to have as much of it as they can take. I want them to be flooded by it..." I let myself trail off, realizing how silly I sound. And how sincere. Because I am. It's all I want for the people I love—Taylor, Harrison, maybe even Miles here. I want them to have as much love as they can stand. I want them to be bowled over, buried in love. I want to see them thrive in it.... "Because if I see that, maybe I'll know I can survive it, too," I say. I pause, waiting for him to mock me. My own fault for opening up to Miles of all people, but I suppose we are friends of a kind.

"Well, if that's what you want...," Miles says, putting his hand on my shoulder. "Then that's what I want, too." He takes a deep breath as I park across the street from Taylor's place. "I kind of want..."

"Oh, please don't ask me to find you a girlfriend tonight," I say, hoping he's not about to get all sincere, too. I think I just used up our mutual limit for the night.

He laughs. "What? No."

"I mean, I will. But not tonight, okay?"

He laughs harder, shaking his head. "I wasn't going to...just..."

I open the door and we get out. Miles is still laughing as we walk to the door.

Inside, Taylor has done the best she can with the decor. There are pink streamers up, and some pink eco-friendly mushroom-foam balls she's covered in faux flowers and sprayed with opalescent paint, then hung from the ceiling in the living room in different combinations, like the flower chandeliers from the museum. They don't quite match beige, but they distract from it, which I suppose is the best anyone can hope for. She has bottles of alcohol lined up on the side table in the living room, along with a big stack of red plastic cups. And people are already here, enjoying. I guess our lateness isn't as fashionable as I'd hoped.

"I need to find Harrison," I say to Miles, by way of saying I'll see him later. I'm sure he has his own friends to mingle with. So I'm surprised when he follows me to the bar. I need a drink before I let Harrison down, but Miles is driving us back, so he shouldn't drink.

"Just one," he says when I raise an eyebrow at him. "I'm doing it now so it'll be out of my system when I need to drive us home."

"What do you even want one for?" I ask, pouring us both screwdrivers and adding a touch of grenadine and a cherry apiece. "You rarely drink."

"Just nerves," he says, taking his cup and toasting it with mine.

"What's wrong with your nerves?" I ask, then drink.

He keeps drinking, and behind him, Taylor comes up to us, leading a handsome guy by the hand.

"Hey, guys," she says, beaming at me especially. "This is West's brother, Andre. Andre, this is Miles and Emmett. Emmett is going to Stanford next year, with you."

I reach out my hand and smile at him. He's even better-looking in person, the moody art student vibe, but a little cleaner, a little more cheerful. He has a wonderful smile, and as he leans in to shake my hand, I smell what I think must be ivy on him, green and fresh. Cologne, probably. Did he wear it for me? Taylor did say she'd been selling me hard.

"It's wonderful to meet you," he says, his voice low and smooth. "Taylor and West have said so many good things."

"About you, too," I say, smiling.

"I'll just let you two talk," Taylor says, her grin so large it might pop off. "Miles, come with me, I need help in the kitchen."

She leads Miles away and Andre smiles at me again. He's got stubble, and the sides of his head are nearly shaved, but long natural coils are on top. "So what are you drinking?" he asks. "It's a cool color. This room needs it."

I laugh. "Taylor's parents do not share her artistic

eye," I say. "And it's just a screwdriver. A little grenadine as an excuse to put a cherry in."

"Can I have a sip?"

I admit my body tingles a little the way he asks it, so I reach out and hand him my glass. He drinks, then hands it back.

"Nice," he says. "Not too sweet. It's good to be able to mix drinks in college. All the guys will love you for it."

"Really? That easy?"

"Well, that and you're good-looking."

I laugh. "I'm sure many people at Stanford are good-looking, if present company is an example."

"Oh no," he says. "I'm the exception. Handsomest one there."

"Is that so?"

"Yeah, we took a vote and everything."

"And yet you're hitting on me, a mere high school senior."

"Well, like I said, no one else there is very good-looking."

I laugh. "So, what do you study there?"

"Architecture. I just did a study abroad actually."

"So you and West both have a love of art, just different."

"Exactly." He sips his drink again, his lips wet against the rim of the cup, and I'm about to say something else, keep the banter going, but behind him, I see the front door open, and Clarke walks in. I manage not to frown, in case Andre misinterprets it, but then Clarke drags in another guy. They're holding hands. He looks familiar, like maybe I've seen him on KamerUhh.

I need to find Harrison. This will devastate him. Clarke is so tacky doing this, too, trying to prove something, maybe. He sees me and waves, his hand still linked with the other boy's, his face somehow triumphant, nasty. I smile back.

"I need to go find a friend," I tell Andre. "I'm so sorry, impending social disaster."

"I remember high school," he says. "You'll come back?"

"Yes," I say, throwing him a real smile before turning around and looking for Harrison. I can't believe I've been flirting with some college boy instead of looking for him. I'm a terrible friend.

I spot him on the sofa, talking to one of the girls from the environmental club. He's holding a glass but spilling it a little. How many has he had?

"…so I just say you should use three times the amount," the girl is saying. "Then the next one tastes better."

"It does!" Harrison says, excitedly, his drink sloshing again. I sigh—maybe this will make it easier. "Emmett!" he says, suddenly noticing me, thrilled. "This is Lindsey, she made me some drinks, she's got this whole philosophy about alcohol, and I think, I think she might be onto something."

"Could be," I say, smiling politely at Lindsey. "Could I borrow you for a moment? We need to talk."

"All right," he says, getting up, then almost falling back onto the sofa, then pushing himself up by the armrest. "Can you believe this is my first time drinking anything other than wine at Passover?"

"I actually can," I say, taking him by the arm and leading him out of the living room and upstairs. I see Clarke in the kitchen and block Harrison from seeing him as we pass by. There's a guest bedroom up here no one ever goes in, and I drag him into that.

"Whoa now, Emmett," he says, smiling at the bed. "I'm trying to date Clarke now, remember? We have a deal. Did you see his KamerUhh video last night?" He pulls out his phone. "That Speedo again. He is so hot."

"Listen," I say, sitting him down on the bed. I look at him. He's smiling, innocent, sweet. He's handsome, too, and a nice guy. Clarke is really a fool.

I swallow. I need to tell him. "That's what we need to talk about. I'm afraid Clarke isn't really interested in you." Tear off the Band-Aid.

His face looks confused, but then it ripples, turning down, his smile slouching.

"Oh," he says, finally.

"He's a narcissist, more interested in KamerUhh views than actual looks or personality."

"I don't have enough followers to date?" He looks up

at me, and his eyes are watery. "I didn't think that mattered. I would have been more…"

"It doesn't!" I put my hands on his shoulders. "Only to Clarke, and you can do better."

"I really liked him," he says, crying for real now.

I wrap my arms around him and let him cry for a little. He hugs me back.

"Am I unattractive?" he whispers, still hugging me.

"No, not at all," I say. "Otherwise I never would have…"

"I don't feel attractive right now." He pulls back. His eyes are red, a little bleary, but he makes himself smile, which is good. "Can you make me feel attractive?" He leans forward and kisses me, and for a moment, I kiss him back before pulling away.

"Harrison, no, you're drunk, and you made me promise not to do this anymore, because you want a real boyfriend."

"I want you," he says, putting his hand on my thigh. "I want to feel you again. I want you to tell me I'm hot."

"You are hot."

"Then come on," he says, his hand drifting farther up my leg. "I'm horny and lonely and I've just been rejected because I'm not online enough."

"You want a boyfriend," I say, trying to keep my tone sympathetic. "And you're drunk and rejected and confused. It's emotionally messy."

"It was messy from day one, Emmett. We have sex, you seem to like me, and I like you, maybe had feelings for you, but you won't date, so you try to find me a boyfriend who doesn't want me.... It's already messy, Emmett. It's always been messy."

He maybe had feelings for me. I suspected it, of course, but I really didn't want him to say it. I didn't want to have to be the bad guy who likes him back but... not like that.

"Oh." He leans back, closing his eyes. "I just said something."

"No you didn't," I say quickly, erasing it. "And you don't have to worry. I actually already have another guy in mind for you."

His eyes open and he looks at me, confused. "You do?"

"He's perfect, trust me." Handsome, flirty, sincere, probably has chemistry with everyone. He's exactly what Harrison needs. He can take care of Harrison.

"Then why didn't you set me up with him?"

"I just met him," I say, standing up. True, it means giving up Andre myself, but that's for the best, too, because I don't want to break my no romance before twenty-five rule. I was never going to. It's much better this way.

"All right," Harrison says, a little dazed. He stands. He's less wobbly.

I lead him back downstairs and pour him a cup of iced coffee from the fridge (Taylor didn't put it out, but this is an emergency and it's me) and make him down it, then a glass of water.

"You feeling better?" I ask.

"Well, I've still been rejected for not being online enough and confessed I caught feelings for my former fuckbuddy turned matchmaker, so I'm not sure I like how much more aware of all that I am, because it's mortifying, but I feel less drunk."

"Seriously," I say, brushing his hair out of his face. "Forget what you told me. You don't even like me that much."

He laughs. "No?"

"No. You just think you do, because I'm good-looking and nice."

"That's a good start."

"You deserve more."

He looks at me, surprised, and then he frowns a little. "Emmett," he starts, but then he closes his mouth for a moment, reconsidering. "Thanks."

"You're my friend. It's my pleasure. Now come meet Andre."

I bring him into the living room, where Andre is chatting with Taylor and West. He looks up and sees me so I march Harrison in front of me, over to them.

"Andre, this is Harrison. Harrison, Andre. Harrison, Andre studies architecture. You like buildings, right?"

"Oh yeah," Harrison says. "I like tall ones."

Over his shoulder, Taylor glares at me.

"Emmett, will you help me in the kitchen?" she asks.

"Sure," I say. "You two keep chatting," I tell them. Andre shoots me a confused look as I walk after Taylor. She turns the moment we get to the kitchen, her hand slamming down on the counter.

"What are you doing?"

"What do you mean?" I ask, all innocence.

"Emmett. We're best friends and have been for years. Andre said you two really hit it off, and now you're marching Harrison in front of him while Clarke strolls around with his new boyfriend. Did you not like Andre?"

"I like him a lot," I say. "But he's boyfriend material. I don't want a boyfriend, remember?"

"You don't want..." She sighs. "That's not what you said."

"It's what I'm saying now," I say, sticking my chin out.

Her mouth turns into a hard line and she folds her arms. "Fine. If you really don't want a boyfriend, then fine."

"I don't," I say, frowning. "And I don't think it's nice of you to get angry at me for it."

"I'm angry at you for lying. You do want a boyfriend. I've seen the way you look at West and me. You practically said so last night. And now you're... what, changing your mind?"

I sigh and look at the counter. There's a bottle of

tequila someone has conveniently moved here. No cups, though, so I march over to the cabinet and take out a plastic glass, and pour myself a shot. I swirl it in my glass before downing it.

"I admit," I say, still looking at the glass, "I sometimes feel a little...lonely. We used to spend a lot of time together, and now you spend it with West, and I'm so happy for you and wouldn't change that for anything. But that's all you're seeing."

"Emmett." She puts her hand on my wrist and I look up. "You know I love you. You know we'll be friends forever, you told me so. That's not what it is. I don't know if you really think that's what it is, and I'll drop it if you want, but last night...you said you wanted someone to kiss in the snow. You don't want that now?"

I think about kissing in the snow again, snowflakes on eyelashes, lips on lips. I shake my head. Harrison needs this more than I do. He deserves it more. "If I did want that, and maybe sometimes I do...not yet."

"Why not?"

"Because our brains aren't—"

"I know that line. Why not? For real?" She squeezes my wrist.

"Because it's more likely to end. And if it ends I'll..." I swallow. That tequila hit me. "...be distracted," I finish. It wasn't what I was really going to say. But it's true enough. "And then I won't get into med school."

"That's why?" Her eyes search me. "Because like I said, a breakup isn't going to be like losing your mom...."

I shake my head, and she goes quiet. She knows I'm holding back. She knows this isn't even about my mom, not exactly. It's about my dad. But I don't want to say anything else out loud. It's a cruel thought. I hate that it even came into my mind.

"I don't want a breakup. The reason isn't important."

"All right." She shrugs. "But I don't know if Harrison is a good fit for Andre."

"Andre is gone in a few weeks; he was just flirting because he wants a holiday hookup. I'm sure anyone will do, and Harrison is wonderful."

"Yeah, but does Harrison only want a few weeks?"

"Oh, hi, Emmett," comes a voice loudly from the kitchen entrance. I look up and see Clarke still holding hands with his date. I wonder if they're surgically attached or if Clarke simply won't let him let go. "This is July," he introduces the man. He's cute, with floppy brown hair, gray eyes. "He goes by HottestMonth on KamerUhh? He's got nine thousand followers."

"That's great," I say, smiling and shaking Hottest-Month's free hand. It's limp, the way a dog hangs its tail between its legs. "How nice to meet you."

"Emmett only has like seven thousand," Clarke says, inaccurately. "You should follow him, babe, he needs the likes."

"Oh, no need. But I'm so glad to meet you. Clarke deserves you," I say.

HottestMonth grunts a little and nods. I'm not sure he speaks at all.

"Let's get back to the living room," I tell Taylor. "I need a mixer for my next drink." She nods. "Nice meeting you," I say, smiling, as we leave Clarke and his date alone.

Except they follow us. Well, Clarke does, dragging HottestMonth with him. I try to ignore them as we head back to Harrison, Andre, and West, who have been joined by Miles.

"It's a really fun exhibit," Harrison is saying. "Pretty."

"It's interesting how they try to decolonialize him, but they fail, of course," West says. "But how could they not, right? Still, the final part, where you can take elements and rearrange them—it lets you do to his work what he did to these landscapes and it's pretty cool."

"You're back," Andre says as we enter the circle. "They're telling me about this weird art exhibit. Apparently *everyone* loves it, and I should see it."

"You should," I say. "Just bring a helmet—lots of falling debris."

"What?"

"Oh," Clarke says, butting into the circle behind us. "And this is Harrison. He's not, like, in our league at all, follower-wise," he says to HottestMonth.

"Really?" I say to Clarke. I glance over at Harrison, who's looking at the floor.

"Clarke, go away," Miles says. "You want to bring some guy to a party, fine. But now you're being intentionally cruel, and that's just tacky."

Clarke rolls his eyes. "Oh, whatever."

I almost want to punch him.

"Clarke, no one here wants to talk to you," Miles says, sounding tired.

Clarke actually sneers, his grip on HottestMonth's hand going white. He's really angry, but I don't know if he'll stop without a reason, so I slip my phone out and start recording him from my hip.

"Hey," Andre says in a soft voice to Harrison. "Let's go to the kitchen and get another drink. I think there's tequila in there."

"Yeah," Harrison says.

Andre links his arm with Harrison and leads him away, while the rest of us glare at Clarke.

"Don't be an asshole to my friends ever again," Miles says.

"Or what?" Clarke says. "*He* was an asshole to me first," he says, nodding at me.

"What?" I glare. "I just told you I wasn't interested...."

"Yeah, because you wanted to set me up with that loser."

"You said your followers want you with a boyfriend,"

I say, hoping he'll go on about using them for prestige again. "Harrison is—"

"Oh please, as if my vapid followers would want to see me make content with some nerd. You know I'm better than that. I need genuine likes, not pity likes."

"You misinterpreting things isn't my fault, Clarke," I say, the tequila in me making my voice a little less than nice. "And as to your question: Or what? If you bother Harrison again, I'll simply post this video of you calling your followers vapid." I hold up my phone. "Tell me, how do you think that'll affect your follower count? Or make people view your new couple's content?" I let my eyes run down his arm to where it meets HottestMonth's. He's pulling away now, but Clarke's grip is iron.

"It's funny you even care about KamerUhh views anyway," Miles adds, that superior smirk playing on his lips. "I thought all the real influencers moved to VDO months ago. KamerUhh is what my mom uses."

Clarke's mouth opens like he's been slapped, and for a moment, he's silent, and I let myself smile. Then he lifts his nose in the air and sneers at each of us in turn. "This party sucks anyway," he says before marching out, dragging poor HottestMonth with him.

"Damn," West says. "I don't think I've ever seen Miles or Emmett go all mama bear like that before."

Taylor laughs. "Last year he punched a freshman who called me an…impolite word."

"I didn't punch him," I say quickly. "I simply made a fist and a face, and that was scary enough to him that he backed up and tripped on the pavement. Hit his head."

"The face you made was like being punched," Taylor says. "I saw it. If you ever made it at me, I'd fall backward, too."

"Well, you don't ever have to worry about that," I say quickly, taking her hand and kissing it. "I love you. I love all of you. Even you, Miles."

"Yeah?" Miles asks, smiling weirdly. "Well, then hopefully you won't hate me when I tell you something...." He takes a deep breath, then starts laughing. "I don't know why I'm so nervous," he says, shaking his head, staring at the ground, still laughing. "I mean...it's you, all of you, so...I'm into guys—I'm queer."

For a moment, it's like all the sound in the room has gone out in a burst of static. I smile. I'm happy for him. That's what a nice person would feel.

"Oh, honey!" Taylor says, immediately giving him a hug. "I'm so happy for you. It's way cooler."

I watch them hug, Taylor so joyful for him, but for some reason, my whole body is ice.

How could he not tell me? He's been my friend for years. He saw me come out. He could have...we could have...I take a deep breath. No. I won't make this all about me. That's not nice. He's a condescending asshole, but he's my friend, too, my oldest friend, and now he just did the thing I know, I *know*, is scary even when it shouldn't be. So I reach out and give him a hug, too.

"Welcome to the club," I say. It's lame, but for some reason, I can't think of anything right to say. Anything perfect. And I still feel...shocked. Fooled, maybe. Like I've been missing something right under my nose for years.

"Thanks," he says. He takes another deep breath, wipes his eyes. "I know it's not a big deal. I mean, I have two moms. But...like...yeah. It's scary!"

"It is," Taylor says. "But now it's awesome." She raises her glass.

"Yeah," Miles says. "It kinda is. I was waiting for my mom to get back to tell her, so I could tell them together, first, in person. That felt important. And now...I've told you guys."

"You should tell everyone," West says. "I mean, I can't welcome you to the club, but I can say it's awesome being yourself, right?" He reaches out and gives Miles a hug.

"Thanks," Miles says. "But you're right. I gotta tell everyone. I mean, I will. I don't want to hide it or anything, it's just...a lot of people. So don't feel like it's a secret. You can tell anyone."

"Ooooh, get the gay gossip out?" Taylor asks. "Then we'd better tell Georgia. She's over there—come on." She links her arm through Miles's and offers her other to me.

"I'm actually going to go get more tequila," I say, keeping my voice cheerful. "I'll be back in a sec."

I turn around and walk to the kitchen. Why do I feel...off? A little sick? I think about those blood tests again. I'll ask Dad to run something more comprehensive tomorrow. Just in case. Blood tests don't spot a lot of things. You need a full genetic workup. Someone needs to study every cell. Find out what's wrong with me. Why I'm not happy for my friend.

In the kitchen, Harrison is grinning, talking to Andre, who's leaning over him, flirty. Harrison glances over at me and nods, and I pour myself another shot of tequila and drink it. Then pour myself another. Then I head back to the living room, so I don't look unsupportive. Because I'm not. Of course I'm not. I just must be coming down with something.

By the time I get back to them, Georgia is hugging Miles so tight it looks like his head might pop off. I smile. Because he's happy and out now, and I'm happy for him. This weird pit in my chest, both like there's a hole in me and like the hole is heavier than lead—that's something else, something wrong with me, a stomach bug maybe. I'm nice. I'd never feel anything but happy for Miles.

"Fuck," Georgia is saying as I approach. "John is going to be so sad he missed this. If he didn't meet someone in Paris, I'm totally setting you two up." My stomach churns a little.

"Oh, that's okay," Miles says, pulling away. "I know John, I don't think he's really my type."

Georgia laughs and slaps him on the shoulder. "That's hilarious. I'm just so happy for you, though. You have to join the Queer Alliance."

"Yeah." Miles nods at that. "Maybe I will." He looks over at me, and I smile brightly, but he flinches and looks away. I feel angry. Why do I feel angry? I should definitely make sure Dad tests my blood . . . well, after the alcohol is out of my system. Tomorrow. Because something is wrong.

I sidle up next to Taylor and we watch Georgia coo some more before hugging Miles again.

"I'm just so happy for you," she says. "Welcome." I think she's on the verge of tears. She's genuinely so happy for him. Why aren't I? I go back to the kitchen and get more tequila, and as I pour myself another drink, I spot Andre handing his phone to Harrison, who enters his number. That should make me feel good, too, it's what I wanted, right? A nice guy for Harrison. I do a shot and pour myself another. The world is a little softer now. I don't usually drink that much but I know the signs, so I have some water, to stave off a hangover. I don't mind the tipsiness. Everyone is entitled to feel a little more at ease from time to time. Dad deals with his anxieties by taking my blood. Me drinking a little too much is surely healthier than that.

"Did you see?" Harrison says, suddenly next to me. "He asked for my number!"

"I saw," I say, grinning. "I'm so happy for you."

"I mean, I know he's only here for break, but he seems really nice."

"Yeah, I thought you'd like him." I put my hand on the counter. The room is swaying a little.

"You all right?" He glances at my hand, and then at the plastic cup I'm holding.

"I'm great. Miles came out! Did you hear?"

"What?" His eyes go wide. "I need to go congratulate him. I mean, I know you don't like him much, but he's always been so nice to me."

"Of course," I say. "And I don't not like him...I mean...don't say that. We've been friends forever. He's just annoying."

"Oh yeah. That's all I mean. I just mean...not like you used to, right?"

My eyebrows rise. "No, not like that. This doesn't reinvigorate the old crush or anything. Dating him would be like asking to be lectured constantly. Do you like him like that?"

He shrugs. "I mean, he's hot, and I think he's really sweet. But I like Andre, and he has my number now, so..." He shakes his head. "Besides, Clarke is one thing, but I'm totally out of Miles's league, right?"

"You can have any man you want," I say, and swallow,

because I believe it, I just don't want him to like Miles that way. It feels...uncomfortable. Icky. I've slept with Harrison, I don't want Miles sleeping with him, too.

He grins. "You're such a good friend to me, Emmett." He reaches out and squeezes my hand. "Even after what a wreck I was before. Thank you."

"Of course," I say.

"I'm going to go congratulate him."

He walks out just as Georgia comes in and pours herself a drink. She looks over at me, squinting.

"So...Miles. How are you feeling about that?" she asks, sipping from her drink.

"Great, of course," I say. "So happy for him."

"Well, yeah, but...I mean, John came out like...six months after I did? But we were friends before that. And I remember I felt a little, like...angry. Because we could have gone through it together. Because I'd trusted him with it but he hadn't trusted me yet."

I nod. I do sort of feel that way, but I'm not going to tell her that. "Well, I'm just happy for him. Maybe I had a little too much to drink."

"I'm sure that's it."

"And it's not like we're that close anymore. He got all condescending."

Georgia laughs. "Sure. *He's* definitely the condescending one." She sips her drink. "Have some water," she says. "And I know you're happy for him, really. It's just…you're allowed to feel lots of stuff, and if you want to talk to someone about it, you can talk to me, you know. That's all I'm saying. You don't have to have the perfect reaction all the time with me."

I raise an eyebrow. "Are you saying I'm not perfect?"

She laughs. "I would never. You're just so used to knowing everything, being in control…and now you're drunk and someone surprised you! It's like you're Opposite Emmett."

"You're right," I say. She is. That makes perfect sense. "You're really right. Sometimes I don't handle surprise as well as I could. Or lack of control."

"Have some water, then." She takes my cup and fills it from the tap. "You look a little green."

"It's the lighting," I say.

She laughs and walks away.

I drink some water as she leaves and watch the rest of the party come in and out of the kitchen. It's a good party. At some point, someone turns on some music, and I dance with Taylor and have a rum and Coke, and pretty soon I'm feeling fine again. Harrison was right—tequila is not for me. Miles is queer, and I'm happy for him. Harrison and Andre hit it off, and I'm happy for them. It's a good night for everyone. Everything is going great.

I'm sad when Miles taps me on the shoulder as I'm swaying to the music and asks if I want to go. I know he's my ride, but part of me just wants to crash here. But then I look over at Taylor and West making out very passionately on the sofa and realize everyone else is gone already, so yes, it's probably time we leave, too.

"Bye," I say to Taylor and West, who ignore me, still embracing passionately. Suddenly the pink foam balls from the ceiling fall, one ball pulling another down, and another, like falling dominoes, cascading around them like a spring shower. They don't even notice. Definitely time to leave.

Outside the air is fresh and smells like palm trees, green and watery, and I feel so loose, so fluid. I get in the car and lie back in the passenger seat as Miles drives us home.

"You have a good time?" Miles asks. "I don't think I've ever seen you drink so much."

"Midterms and the carnival," I say. "I deserved a rest."

"Okay." He takes a turn. The streets are empty, dark. "Nothing to do with me then, right?"

"What?" I ask, staring at my reflection in the window.

"I just mean, you seemed kind of weird when I came out. Maybe I'm imagining it."

"It's not all about you, Miles," I say. It comes out meaner than I meant, so I laugh, to cover the tone up, but it just makes the silence that follows more awkward. "I mean, I was surprised. Why didn't you ever tell me? When I was going through all my coming-out stuff…it would have been nice to go through it with a friend."

I look over at him, and he smiles a little, his eyes on the road. "Now who's making it all about him?"

"Well, you asked," I say. "I just mean…it was kind of lonely until I met Taylor. And now it feels like it didn't have to be."

"I didn't know," he says. "If I could have made you less lonely, you know I would have."

"You didn't know?" I ask.

"Yeah. I guess I didn't really have any sort of…anything for people. Like, I liked people, and I pictured myself getting married one day, and all that, but there was never a person. Just an idea, and the sexy parts… I didn't feel them very strongly? And then one day, I'm looking at this guy, and he says something. Something kind of weird and kind and annoying, and right in that moment, I wanted to kiss him. I wanted to put my mouth on his and bring his body close and…well, a lot of other things after that. It was almost out of nowhere? Not really, when I think back on it. But also sort of? It's hard to explain."

"So there's one guy," I say.

He shrugs. "I don't know. Maybe I'll feel that for another guy someday, or a girl, or someone nonbinary. But clearly, I'm not straight."

"So are you going to tell the guy?"

He laughs. "No. No, no, no."

"Why not?"

"He wouldn't like it."

I sit up. "Did you fall for a straight guy?"

He stares at the road a moment. "Let's not get into it."

I laugh. "Don't worry. We've all been there. Straight-boy crushes are the worst." I remember mine—on Miles. So I guess it wasn't as much of a straight-boy crush as I thought.

He pulls the car in in front of his place and shakes his head. He looks over at me, and I remember why I had a crush on him, too. He's hot.

"You know," I say. "If you want, since you're new to all this, I could show you the ropes?"

"Ropes?" he asks.

"Sexually," I say. "Just for fun. I know I'm not your straight guy. But you can imagine I am, I don't care."

His face goes flat, like I've insulted him, and I frown.

"Wow," I say, "okay, sorry."

"I just…that's not for me, Emmett."

"I just thought we could have some fun, you could learn some things for when you have a boyfriend, sorry."

"I'm just not…I'm a romantic, Emmett. I think I'm demisexual. You know? I only really feel for a guy when we've clicked emotionally."

"Sure," I say. "And we've been friends how long?"

"You know that's not how it works." He sighs. "Emmett, you don't even like me. You call me conde-scending behind my back."

I clench my jaw. I wonder who told him that.

"Your voice isn't as quiet as you think it is," he says, as if he hears me asking it.

"Well, it's not like you like me, either," I say, opening the door of the car. "You've always made that very clear." I hop out onto the driveway.

"That's not true," he says, "And I just told you something major and...come on, get back in the car, we'll talk."

He's right. He did just reveal something. And I'm happy for him, I am, but...this has been a long time coming. "I'm happy for you," I say, turning around. "But let's just call this what it is. Ex-friends whose families are close. It's fine. We can be civil like we always have been. I won't make my dad stop seeing your moms. I don't think he could...." I take a deep breath. "I'll see you later, Miles."

I close the car door and walk across the street to my place. Inside, the lights are out. Dad is already asleep. So I go up to my room, get in the shower, and for some reason, I cry for a while.

chapter nine

THE NEXT MORNING, I FEEL KIND OF CRUSTED OVER. MY SKIN FEELS dry, my eyes thick. I drink some water and take my temperature. No fever. I'll have Dad do some blood work. I'm sure I have something. That would explain how I feel this morning, and how I felt last night. Why I cried in the shower, too. Physiological effects of viruses and infections can easily cause extreme emotional shifts. Your body controls your mind, just like your mind controls your body. Emotional trauma can make you shiver, but shivering from a fever can be emotionally taxing.

Certainly I wasn't crying because of rejection. I think sex with Miles would be fun, but if he wasn't feeling it, that's fine. His loss, really. Maybe I felt a little upset because of our tiff, but it's not like we haven't traded worse barbs. I'm sure everything will be normal by tomorrow.

Downstairs, Dad has made superfood spelt-and-blueberry pancakes, which are extremely good. I have several before I ask him to test my blood, which he happily does.

"I thought we could decorate for the holidays today," he says as my blood fills the little tube. "Maybe go pick out a tree?"

"That sounds nice," I say. And it does. Picking out the tree, weirdly, was always Mom's favorite part. There's a tree farm about an hour away and we'd drive up and spend hours just looking them over, but a few years after she died, I found a tree rental place, where they give you a tree in a pot, and you return it after, and they plant it back in the ground. Much more eco-friendly, so we changed to that. Plus it was nice going to a different tree farm. At the old one, I could always feel Mom's absence.

So I shower and dress while he mails my blood sample in to the lab, but the truth is, I'm feeling a lot better today. Maybe it really was the tequila. I really am happy for Miles. A little offended he turned me down for some sexy fun, but if he's demi, then it's just not for him, and it's not about me, really, so it's all fine. Still, I turn over what he said yesterday and wonder if maybe my pushing the idea of us having no-strings sex when he was clearly declining offended him. In which case a simple apology will settle it. I'm sure everything will go back to normal soon.

We drive out to the tree farm and walk up and down

the aisles of potted firs and spruces, most a little taller than me, in huge pots. The pot can be changed, but since coming here, Dad and I like to make a game of picking the perfect combination, ready-made.

"I like the tree," Dad says, examining a fir. "Looks robust. But the pot..." He looks down. "A little sad, don't you think?"

"Very." I nod. "How about this one? The pot is blue, which is a nice nod to my Jewish side."

"No, no, look at this empty patch."

It takes us forty minutes before we decide on a healthy-looking pine in a pretty white pot. Then another forty minutes to maneuver it into the car—you can't just strap it to the roof when it's got a heavy pot that needs to be on a surface. So we put it on the floor in the back, the top of it reaching out through the sunroof, and drive back slowly so the tip doesn't break off. At home, we now have to get it out of the car, which for some reason is much harder than getting it in, and bring it to the living room. Once we've put it down, I collapse onto the sofa, and Dad into an armchair, both of us catching our breath.

"I swear the trees get bigger every year," Dad says. "Or the pots get heavier."

"They might. Maybe we should start taking pot weight into account."

"At least we're having a good meal tonight. Jasmine and Priyanka invited us over."

I frown.

"What?" Dad asks. "I assumed it was all right. You want to see them, don't you?"

"Yes," I say. "Yes, I just was thinking of spending the night doing nothing. But this is much better."

Dad laughs. "I should think so."

I laugh with him. Everything will be fine with Miles, and I really do want to see Priyanka and Jasmine.

After a brief lunch of reheated healthy tacos (they weren't too bad, actually) and plenty of green tea, we start decorating. There are ornaments of all kinds for the tree—Jewish ones, like dreidels, and plenty of medical ones, even a financial manager one: a money clip holding mistletoe. And then there are the more personal ones; stuff my dad's family has passed down forever, like the Woodhouse family crest from England, and photos of my grandparents. And there are classic ornaments—glass balls, twinkling stars. Finally, there are the ones I made as a child... Popsicle sticks with googly eyes. Dad loves those. He picks up a Popsicle-stick Star of David covered in blue-and-silver glitter.

"When did I make that?" I ask, hanging a more traditional white orb on a branch.

"Oh, your mother made this," Dad says, smiling at it.

"What?" I look back at the ornament. It definitely looks like it was made by a child.

"When we first moved in together, an apartment down

in LA. She'd never had a Christmas tree before; she felt"—he tilts his head—"guilty. But excited. Which made her feel more guilty. So she said if she was going to have a Christmas tree—and I offered not to, but she insisted—but if she was going to have one, then some of the ornaments had to be Jewish. So she wasn't…cheating, I guess."

"So she made that?" I ask, walking closer and taking the glitter star from him. "How old was she?"

"Oh…we moved in after college, so twenty-two?"

"Twenty-two…" I knew my parents met in college, but for some reason I had assumed they didn't really become a thing until they were done with grad school. Priyanka always says medical school was so busy that she and my mom barely had time for a social life. And they didn't get married until Mom was thirty-three. "Wait, so when did you start dating?"

"Um…we were nineteen. Your mother might have been eighteen—about your age."

"My age?" I almost drop the ornament. I guess this shouldn't really be surprising. I've seen photos, and they always looked young together, but I guess…I just thought that was because Dad looks so old now.

"What?" Dad laughs. "Just realizing that?"

"I guess…," I say, hanging the ornament on the front center of the tree. "But then…how did you know? I mean, Mom was a doctor, she knew your brains weren't done developing. You weren't old enough to be yourselves yet, much less know who you wanted to spend the rest of your life with."

Dad shakes his head and brings over an ornament I remember making with Mom, a Star of David but painted green and decorated with red balls of glitter, like a wreath.

"We weren't thinking about that, Emmett," he says. "We were in love. We weren't thinking about it ending. Love doesn't make you imagine an ending."

"But what if it ended…" I trail off. It did end. Terribly. "Knowing what you know now," I say, the room very quiet, "would you still…?"

Dad turns to look at me, shocked, and blinks away tears before turning back to the tree and hanging the wreath star next to Mom's ornament. Then he takes both my shoulders in his hands and looks me in the eye.

"In a heartbeat," he says. "Without hesitation. Your mom and I had years together. Amazing years. I would never give those up."

"Even if it meant you wouldn't have the pain of…"

Dad scoffs, shakes his head. "Pain. What's pain next to love?"

"But love ends," I say.

"No," Dad says, dropping his hands. "It doesn't. It changes. But if you think for a moment that I don't still love your mother and she doesn't still love me…" He turns back to the box and pulls out a little framed photo ornament—Mom holding baby me. "Love changes. And sometimes there's pain. A bad breakup means maybe you won't see someone again, or that you'll hate them, too. But past you—he loved them. And that love made him better. Even if maybe it turned sour or ... died." He says the last word in a whisper, then hangs the ornament on the tree. "Flowers die, but that doesn't make them less beautiful," he tells me, then turns around, a sad smile on his face. "Come on, no need to be so morbid today. We're decorating a tree, for Christ's sake." He laughs. "Literally, for Christ's sake."

I laugh, too, even though it's not a great joke, and I take out another ornament, a little snowman I drew on a shell. Dad is wrong, of course. He needs to tell himself it was worth it, but the pain he's in, the pain he feels all the time ... it can't have been worth it. Can it?

I hang up the shell and look at the photo of Mom. Maybe Mom was worth it. But surely no one else could be.

That night, we bring a bouquet from the garden and a bottle of wine over to Miles, Priyanka, and Jasmine's place. Even outside the door, it smells amazing; garlic, spices, oil, and butter. I realize how much I've missed eating food for pleasure and not to fight free radicals. I mean, I make myself quick simple meals I like, and Dad's healthy meals range from cardboard to perfectly fine, but from the smell alone I know that this is culinary extravagance. Miles opens the door, and I can tell immediately his smile is forced.

"Hey," he says. "Come on in."

I hand him the wine, and he nods but won't meet my eyes. I really don't see what he has to remain so annoyed about. If I can manage his rejection, surely he can understand if I was offended. But I guess that's classic Miles: I've somehow lowered myself in his eyes, either through my drunkenness or my offer of sex or both, and now he can't even deign to look at me. Well, fine. I'm not here for him anyway.

"Emmett!" Priyanka calls out when she sees me. Their house is much more open than ours, with a huge central kitchen, with a skylight over it, perfect for filming, while the rest of the house circles it—living room on one side, dining on the other, and on each side a hallway to a bathroom and a bedroom. You can see practically anywhere in the house from anywhere else, although it's large enough that you can't see well. And they've decorated it beautifully, with sapphire tile in the kitchen, and greens and gold everywhere else. A glass orb chandelier hangs over the dining room table, and the sofas are tan leather. I've always loved the style here. It feels like camping, somehow. Or glamping, I suppose, as there are no bugs, there's indoor plumbing, and it's actually enjoyable.

Priyanka runs over and gives me a hug, and then

hugs Dad, too. Jasmine is behind the stove, cooking, and Knight is here as well, filming her as she cooks.

"Should we not talk?" I whisper to Priyanka, nodding at Knight.

"Oh no, they just want the visuals. Then, if you're all right with it, maybe some photos for the cookbook?"

"Oh," I say. "I didn't dress up or anything."

"No, no," Knight says, hearing us. "Just casual eating things. Family photos. We don't want anything too polished." They look up from the camera to me. "Besides, you look great."

I smile. "Thank you, so do you." They do. Their leather jacket is slung over a dining room chair, and they're in a gray tank top that shows off their excellently muscled arms, and a bit of hair on the sliver of skin above their waist.

The corner of their mouth turns up as they go back to filming Jasmine.

"Well, I didn't know this was just so you could use us in your book," Dad says, teasing.

"Never," Priyanka says. "Just multitasking." She lowers her voice to a whisper. "Apparently she's a month behind on the book."

"I can hear that!" Jasmine shouts. "And I was doing the work of two mothers for a year! Being only a month behind is good."

Priyanka grins. "Yes, and thank you for that, sweetie."

"I'm not saying it's your fault," Jasmine quickly adds.

"You were doing much more important work than a cookbook, and I wanted you to be doing it...just saying I didn't prepare as much as I should have." As she says this, she grabs a pair of spice jars without looking and shakes them into the pan she's stirring, and she does it artfully, making long powdery lines of burgundy and yellow in the air before they fall into the pan.

Priyanka laughs. "That's you—unprepared." She goes back over to Jasmine and kisses her squarely on the lips, squeezing her around the waist. Jasmine grabs another spice but this time as she's about to add it to the pan, Priyanka squeezes her again and her hand holding the spice shakes too much, sending the yellow powder up into the air and then falling down on them like rain. Jasmine bursts out laughing. "Now we taste like curry," she says.

"Don't care," Priyanka says, kissing her again.

"Well, now I wish I were recording for sound," Knight says.

"Don't put that up," Jasmine says to them, shaking her head. "Some things are just for us. Now this needs to sit for a few minutes...." She puts a lid over the pan. "So let me go make sure I'm not overly spiced for the photos. Miles, Emmett, can you set the table?"

"Sure," I say.

"Actually, Miles can handle that with Henry," Priyanka says. "Emmett, you come help me find a nonalcoholic drink for you two...."

"Okay," I say, following her downstairs to their wine cellar. It's not as large as upstairs, but it's beautifully laid out. Jasmine knows her wines as well as she does her food.

"So," Priyanka says, looking at the shelves. "How are you?"

"What?" I ask, feeling like the question is pointed. And she brought me down here where no one can hear us. I hope Miles didn't say anything about last night. "I'm fine."

"It's just...your dad said something about trying to take your blood?"

"Oh." I laugh with relief. "Yes, he tries that. He's always tried that. Well...since Mom died." I look at the shelf devoted to nonalcoholic wines and liquors. Not root beer or anything, but fancy crafted bottles of special brews.

"I knew he got his nursing degree...," Priyanka says. "But...taking your blood without your consent isn't okay, Emmett. You know that, right?"

"Oh." I turn around, quickly shaking my head. "No, no, Pri, he would never. He asks a lot, but I only let him when I'm actually feeling sick. It reassures him, and it reassures me, because all he does is send it out to a lab, and I know they're not going to see things in it that aren't there, right?"

She nods. "Right. Well...okay. Still...I feel like since I've been gone, he's gotten worse. Maybe he should be seeing a psychologist? I can...try to recommend that, if you want."

I laugh. "It probably couldn't hurt...but it's been

like this since Mom died. I mean, it's a reaction to Mom, right, so—"

"Well," she interrupts, pulling out a bottle of T. Totalle and showing it to me, "that wasn't your mom's death. I mean...you remember, he was like this before, too. I think it's why he started dating your mom—she was premed and he was a hypochondriac. Sorry, that makes it sound cheap. They loved each other wildly. But she could always calm him down when he was freaking out. And I think after she died it came back, but I was there, and I guess I didn't think about that when I left, so it just feels like—"

"Whoa," I say. "Stop. No. This isn't your fault, and he's not that bad, and I can manage him." I take a deep breath and put back the T. Totalle and grab a bottle of Nectaryn instead. "I think this is the one Jasmine said works best with spice, and it smelled like spice up there." I turn the bottle around, showing her, but she keeps looking at me, not it. "Maybe a psychologist wouldn't be the worst thing. He never went to one after she died, said he didn't want to take the time away from me. I thought all his health worries were about Mom...and now me about to go to college..."

"Maybe that's making it worse. But it's always been there....He just needs someone to keep him in check, I think. To remind him that he's being too much, instead of letting him take your blood when you feel sick."

"I don't mind it."

"Well…I'll talk to him later. This isn't your job. But thanks for talking to me." She squeezes my shoulder.

"What were they like, together, when they were younger?" I ask. "Mom kept him sane?"

"Oh." She smiles, her eyes miles away. "They were so funny together. They would make each other laugh all the time, and it was infectious—your dad would tell a joke and your mom would laugh and then she'd repeat it and we'd all laugh and then she'd tell a joke…like watching the best kind of romantic comedy."

I nod. "Did things ever fall on them?"

"What?"

"Never mind." I shake my head. "This good?" I hold out the bottle. "I smelled a lot of garlic and I think this is the one Jasmine always grabs for garlicky stuff."

"Good call." She squeezes my arm again, and we start upstairs. "Hey, did Miles talk to you last night?"

I freeze, then remember. "About being queer? Yeah."

"Isn't it great?" she says, smiling at me in a weird way. "He's family now! I mean, obviously, he's my son, he was always family. But now capital *F*."

"What?" I ask.

She laughs as we come back out into the kitchen. "It's old slang. Older than me. How queer people talk about each other. Family."

"I hope you were already talking about me as family," Miles says from the kitchen. "I think being the son of lesbians means I was part of the community even if I wasn't queer."

"Of course it does, baby," Priyanka says, kissing him on the forehead. "But I don't deny being thrilled you're even queerer than that."

He laughs, then looks at me and narrows his eyes. "What were you two talking about down there?"

"Nothing," Priyanka says quickly, and Jasmine reappears, spice-free.

"You didn't change," she says to Priyanka, dusting her off. "We want to look casual in the photos, not crusted."

"I'm going to set up some lights around the dining room," Knight says. "We want casual but...visible. Okay?"

"You're the photography major," Jasmine says.

"And public relations," Knight adds quickly, winking at me. I feel myself grin widely and hear Miles's exasperated sigh.

"All right, go sit down," Jasmine says. "I'm going to bring this over." She opens the lid on the pan and then on a nearby pot and starts moving things from one to the other, throwing in other things as she mixes. I can't keep track, it's a whir of color and smell. On TV, she goes slower, and explains every move she makes, but at home, you can see she's cooking for herself, the way her eyes focus in on every moment, and the small way she smiles as certain sounds happen—a sizzle, a splash. It's like she's hearing poetry in a language no one else understands. Or perhaps writing it.

We go sit down at the table and Knight starts taking photos. They have a camera, not just their phone, for this. "Don't look at me," they say when we turn. Jasmine comes over last and starts dishing out the meal.

"Okay," she says. "So this is a new one. I've made it for myself a few times, but we're testing it. It's like a chili, but the flavors are a mix from Priyanka's ancestral home in southern India and my home state of Georgia, and we're serving it with very garlicky corn bread." She starts dishing out food onto our plates and my mouth starts to water. The chili is in bowls and topped with a little sour cream and it tastes almost like a biryani, but it eats like a chili—filling and thick, and the spice is like both of them—three kinds of fire. Maybe four. I'm grateful for the corn bread, which isn't just sweet and filled with sweet corn flavor but also extravagantly garlicked, crusted with little pieces of browned garlic sticking to it. It helps cut the spice on my tongue but also makes the flavors in the chili pop out more—paprika, cumin, tenderly roasted beef.

"This is magnificent," I say. "Exquisite."

"It came out perfect, sweetie," Priyanka adds.

"Yeah, Mom."

"Spices are good for your immune system," Dad says.

"And they taste good," I say, looking at Priyanka, who smiles, but a little sadly. "Don't forget that part, Dad."

"Yeah!" Dad says. "Sorry. It tastes amazing, Jas."

"You should eat, too," I tell Knight. I hand them a piece of the bread. "This bread is like putting God in your mouth."

Knight smirks at me but takes the bread. Their eyes close with pleasure as they bite into it. "Okay, this needs to go in the book, Jas."

"Yeah," I second. "Wait, is that what you're testing? If it goes in the book?"

"I have most of it figured out, but I thought maybe a few new things…" Jasmine smiles. "You all like it, though?"

"I mean, I haven't tried the chili yet," Knight says.

Jasmine laughs and fills a bowl for them.

"It should, Mom."

"Absolutely," Priyanka says.

"Henry?" Jasmine asks, looking over at Dad, who is dipping his bread in his nearly empty bowl.

"What?" he asks.

"Is this good enough for a cookbook?" Jasmine asks.

"Oh, yes, of course," he says. "You know what it reminds me of? Remember when you and Julie were at the sorority, Pri? And there was that pizza place down the street."

Priyanka beams. "Yes. With the overly fluffy garlic bread. That's what we called it. Overly fluffy garlic bread."

"Well, I think we have a name for this bread, then," Jasmine says. "Overly Fluffy Garlic Corn Bread."

"The chili is amazing, too," Knight says, putting their bowl down and taking another photo.

"I think you have a hit, sweetie," Priyanka says, kissing Jasmine on the forehead.

"Cute," Knight says, snapping a photo. "How long have you two been together anyway? I don't think I know that story."

"Twenty years," Priyanka says quickly. "Met when I was still a resident. She was a sous-chef...where was it?"

"Rhapsody. All the Michelin stars. Chef was a tyrant, though."

"I remember. You had practically chopped your finger off and the whole time you were saying you needed to get back to the kitchen."

"Still have the scar," Jasmine says, showing us her hand. A scar stretches around her left index finger like a ring. "It's my favorite." She gasps. "I should do something with that. A scar...scars..." She stands up and goes to the kitchen, where she has a bunch of notebooks, and starts jotting things down. We all watch and after a moment, she looks up, grinning.

"All right," she says. "Technically, there is a pie. Peach, not a new recipe or anything. But if you're willing to give me"—she tilts her head—"a little over an hour, we can have something never before tasted."

"I always love an experiment," I say.

"I'm game," Priyanka says.

"I was hoping to get some dessert photos," Knight says, and glances at their phone.

"I'm paying you overtime. You have a party or some-thing to go to?" Jasmine asks, already taking out flour and sugar.

Knight looks like they're deciding, then shakes their head. "Nah. I'll stay."

"Great," Jasmine says. "Everyone, have a drink, go outside, look at the stars, I'll try to get this ready as fast as I can."

I look over at Miles, who is stealing another piece of bread. "Want to go outside?" I ask him. "It's nice out."

"That's okay," he says without looking at me.

"I'll go outside with you," Knight says. "I need to go over some of these and it'll be easier without any glare." They hold up their camera. "You can tell me if you don't look good enough in any, and I'll delete them."

"Deal," I say. I could also arrange for the worst ones of Miles to be saved, I think, but... no, that wouldn't be nice. Even if Miles is being even worse than usual right now.

We go out the back door onto the deck. There's a pool out back, and the smells of spices and sugar fade into grass and chlorine. Knight walks out onto the lawn, and I follow, looking up at the stars, hands in my pockets. I start thinking about what Priyanka said, about my dad. A psychologist is an excellent idea. I hope she convinces him.

"You ever see a psychologist?" I ask Knight.

They laugh, low and sexy. "Oh yeah. Since I was fif-teen. Why?"

"Priyanka thinks my father might need one, and I'm inclined to agree."

"He doesn't have one?"

I shake my head.

"Do you?"

I shake my head again.

They let out a low whistle. Shocked? Impressed?

"What?" I ask.

"Just...No, it's not my place. You see a shrink as long as I have, you sort of want everyone to see one, you know? I love it, just a chance to unpack, really think in a way I don't have time for, and with someone who makes me. But what you and your dad need—I couldn't say."

"But you think he does? That I do?"

"I think...Look, I only know what I've heard. But I think watching your wife or mom waste away for a year and then die, and you being so young...yeah. A shrink would be good for both of you." Up close, and without Jasmine cooking around us for once, I notice they have a smell—cologne or deodorant maybe, like oranges, bright and a little bitter. "But like I said, I'm going to think that about everyone."

"Well, Priyanka is going to try to convince him. I hadn't thought about me...." I look at the stars. "I mean, I don't think I need one."

They laugh again. "No?"

I look at them, prepared to glare, but they don't seem

to be laughing at me, exactly. "I just...I think I'm coping well. As well as I can, anyway. And I don't remember the wasting away, not really." I think of Mom, looking like skin and bones, bald, deep circles under her eyes, lying in bed, me snuggled in her arm reading to her. I see it's a sad memory, but it feels warm. Happy. Which is what makes it sad, too, but not in the way Knight might think.

I shake my head. "I think the only reason I'd need one is so I don't—" I stop myself. I was about to say something cruel.

"What?" they ask. They step closer, and the scent of orange grows stronger, warmer.

"I just..." I lower my voice to a whisper. "Promise not to tell?"

"I'll be your shrink training wheels, won't tell a soul," they say.

"I'm afraid of becoming my father."

They chuckle. "That's everyone's fear."

"What?"

"I mean, I'm sorry, I understand what you're saying, but everyone is afraid they'll turn out like their parents." They put their hand on my shoulder and squeeze.

"But it's different with me. I mean...his reacting badly to what happened. To Mom...leaving. I can't fall apart like that."

They look at me, confused—and for a moment, I think, pitying—and I shrug off their hand. "Emmett, if your wife dies…if your mom dies…you're allowed to fall apart. You *should* fall apart."

I nod. They're right, of course. But they're also not quite understanding what I mean. "But I don't want to," I say.

"Well, that seems like something to talk to a real shrink about. But I'd say it's normal not to want pain, but also you gotta remember, pain is unavoidable. But what do I know?" They step away and look up at the stars; then they take their camera, which has been slung around their neck, and hold it up. "Wanna help me pick your best side?"

"Are you saying I have a worse side?" I ask, stepping closer.

They laugh. "Not you. You're perfect."

"I'm glad you finally admitted it," I say, now close enough to smell the orange again. We look over the photos, picking out really good ones and deleting really bad ones. We look really happy together. A family.

"Are you and Miles fighting?" they ask, after we've gone over several dozen photos, moving to a bench near the pool. "He's not meeting your eyes in any of these. Normally he's always looking over at you."

I sigh and roll my eyes. "Not fighting. I don't think so. I said something stupid last night. You know he came out, right?"

Knight nods. "What, you hit on him?"

I don't say anything and they laugh again.

"I was drunk," I say quickly. "And I was just offering

—208—

to...show him the ropes. Which...all right, he did say he thought he was demisexual, and so maybe my pushing that offer was a little disrespectful. But he rejected me, and I'm fine with it, so I don't see the problem."

"Maybe just awkwardness," Knight says. "I mean your best friend says they wanna screw, that's gotta change the dynamic, right?"

"Well, I certainly wouldn't call myself his best friend," I correct. "But no, I don't think that's true. Sex and friendship can go hand in hand, same as sex and romance, or even sex and anonymity. Or do you only sleep with those lucky enough to win your heart?"

They laugh, loudly this time. "Nah, you're right. I screw my friends. But Miles is new to this, Emmett. And not every queer person is like us. Some really do want that romance. I mean, I want romance sometimes. When I date someone, and we're monogamous, then yeah, it's romance. Screwing friends is...different. And even then, usually we have to work out what our friendship is with the sex, what it means. We don't just say 'Now we're friends who have sex' and hop into bed, and then go 'And now we're friends who do not have sex' later. It's not just tidy little labels you switch out, each with a set of rules. You have to negotiate it. Otherwise it gets messy. Hell, it usually does anyway."

"I don't know if that's true. I think it can stay neat if you're neat enough."

"Maybe it doesn't get messy for you, then." They raise

an eyebrow. "Lucky you." They lean back and look up at the sky, the smell of orange growing stronger. "Although, you know, I like the mess. Well...not like. But, y'know, we get to make these relationships up. We're queer. Straight people are basically told from birth the kind of relationships they're supposed to have—straight guys are told they can't be emotional with their friends, and they have to love their wives but joke about what a pain they are, too. Women are supposed to love but also hate their female friends, and love but also hate their husbands. They're trained to be like that. A lot of them are—it takes work to break out. All we have to do is come out. Then we shatter all those ideas, and we get to make everything up—we're friends, but we love each other and have sex, but it's not romantic, or maybe we used to have sex, but we don't, or he's my ex and he's my closest friend in the world...it's messy, but it's ours." They shrug. "Straight people can get there, too, of course, but...a lot don't. We get to make it up the moment we come out and shatter all those ideas we're taught about relationships. If we want, I mean. No offense to the guys who meet and get married and live a happy monogamous life. As long as it's their decision and not just trying to be like straight people. Does that make sense? I dunno, I'm rambling here. But the point is...friends can be more than friends. Maybe it'll be a mess. But then you negotiate your way through that mess. Together. Which makes your friendship stronger."

We're sitting arm to arm, and the camera is in their lap. I can feel the heat of their body through their leather jacket.

"You know, we're friends," I say slowly.

"Something like that," they say; their voice is careful. The orange smell seems to grow stronger, juicier.

"Maybe we can negotiate something," I say.

They're silent for a moment, and I consider the mortification of being rejected twice in as many days.

"Maybe," they say. "But how old are you?"

"I'll be eighteen in March," I say quickly.

"Aries?"

"Yes. Does that pertain to what we're discussing?"

They laugh again. "You're funny. And hot. If you still want to talk about this in March, we can talk about it. But not in front of my boss, who thinks of you as her other son, okay? We'd need to negotiate some boundaries around work-Knight and play-Knight."

"Completely understood. I look forward to March."

"If you change your mind before then, I won't be at all offended."

"I don't know why I would," I say.

We hear the door to the house close with a creak and turn around. Miles is over by the door.

"Mom says dessert is ready," he calls to us.

"Can you go in ahead?" I whisper to Knight. "I should apologize to him again."

"Sure thing," they say, standing up. When they walk away, the smell of orange fades back into chlorine. Miles waits by the door, looking at me impatiently, and I approach slowly, but stop before going inside. It's just the two of us, and Knight was right, he's not meeting my eyes.

"I'm sorry," I say quickly. Apologies are best done politely and to the point. "I was rude last night. We *are* friends, not just family friends. That was a mean lie because I felt rejected—but my offer was impolite. You'd just explained to me how your attraction works, and how it seemed to be uniquely tied to a connection you had, and I completely ignored that. It was disrespectful, and I apologize."

He sighs but still won't look at me. "Emmett, I…" He shakes his head. "It's fine. Don't worry about it."

"Really?" I ask.

He looks up and smiles, but it's small, maybe forced, or a little sad. "Really," he says. "Can we go have dessert?"

I go inside. Maybe he needs more time, but I've done the nice thing, and he knows I'm sorry.

"Okay," Jasmine is saying as she takes something out of the oven. "Get the camera ready, Knight, because I am unveiling my new hopefully amazing dessert: Finger Cut Blondies." She puts a tray down on the counter and we all peer around, Knight shooting photos. It smells amazing—like strawberry shortcake and caramel. The tray looks like a sea of red, with crisp beige cookies in big broken chunks on top.

"What I did was I used a caramel shortcake base for the blondie, then layered on a lot of strawberry jam, and topped it with broken ladyfingers. So it looks like that cut I had on my own lady finger, which *those* lady fingers sewed up." She smiles at Priyanka.

"Lady fingers," Priyanka says, smiling, her eyes tearing up. She kisses Jasmine on the lips. "This is amazing."

"It smells so good," Dad says.

"It's dessert," Priyanka says to Dad, heading him off. "Just enjoy the sweetness."

"I—" Dad starts.

"Just enjoy the sweetness, Dad," I repeat.

"I was going to say I will," Dad says.

Jasmine cuts us each one of the scar blondies and puts it on a plate, and when mine comes I bite into it almost immediately. It's still hot, and it tastes like strawberries but also caramel and the crisp vanilla of the ladyfingers, all of it melting into something warm and sweet and... home, somehow.

"I'm going to recommend serving them with chocolate chip ice cream," Jasmine says, nodding as she eats hers. "But I think they came out pretty good."

Everyone nods and murmurs in agreement, their mouths full, and Jasmine laughs.

"Just goes to show," she says. "If you remember them right, scars can be sweet."

chapter ten

THE LAST WEEK BEFORE BREAK IS MOSTLY JUST ABOUT GETTING tests back and finishing off college applications. Thankfully I don't need to worry about the latter, and the former goes decently. As in pretty much everything except English, because apparently the thesis of my essay had a "somewhat slanted understanding of Jane Austen's text" according to Ms. Levine. She gives me an A-, though, which is good enough that I'm not worried about my GPA. In class, even the teachers goof off, playing games with us that only have a passing relationship to the topics they supposedly instruct us in.

"So John's flight lands Friday night," Georgia tells us at lunch on Wednesday. "So the party will be Saturday. He's going to come over as soon as he's awake and we're going to spend all day just talking and setting up and then he has to have dinner with his parents, so we'll all meet at my place and start the party, and he can enter late, make an entrance as the guest of honor. It's going to be so amazing."

I nod and smile. Miles hasn't sat with us at all this week, so it's just me, her, West, and Taylor, meaning all the focus is on me.

"Sounds great," I say, taking a raspberry from the small bowl of them in front of me and eating it. "I'm sure he'll love it."

"Everyone is going to be there," Georgia says. "Your brother is coming, right?" she asks West.

"Oh yeah. Andre liked hanging out with everyone, so he's game." Taylor nudges him subtly, but not so subtly I don't see it. "And he really wants to see you again, Emmett."

"Oh, does he?" I ask.

Taylor frowns at me. We're not fighting, not exactly, but she's still hoping for me and Andre to hook up, and I'm hoping for Andre and Harrison to hook up, and maybe she feels like there's part of me I'm . . . not indulging. Part of me I'm scared of. And maybe I am, if I'm being honest. When I said it aloud to Knight, that I was afraid of breaking like my father did, it felt right, and what they said felt right, too. Pain is unavoidable. But still . . . I'm sure I'll be able to handle it better once my brain is fully developed. And I'll tell Taylor that, I think. When she asks.

She raises her eyebrow at me, and I realize I'm grinning, so I wiggle my eyebrows and pop another raspberry in my mouth. Then I spot Miles behind her, eating alone and reading, which is ridiculous, so I text him, telling him to come sit with us. He doesn't even take out his phone. He doesn't respond to my text at all that day. Later, at the soup kitchen, Jasmine says he wasn't feeling well, and not even Knight is there, so we cook, just the two of us, and talk about other recipes from the book.

"Tell Miles I hope he feels better," I say, and she nods. But he still doesn't text me back that night. Or Thursday. Or Friday.

Friday, though, I do get a FaceTime from Harrison. I almost assume it's a butt-dial or something when it comes in, but I answer it anyway. I'm only just home from school, my books down on the table. Dad, for once, is home later than me, but he mentioned he'd be late tonight, he had a lot of meetings. He'd said we'd order pizza. I need to time it so I can order from the good place just before he gets home.

But when Harrison calls, I'm so confused I answer, and the picture on my phone immediately goes to him, in his bed. His eyes are red, like he's been crying.

"Harrison?" I ask. "Are you all right?"

He nods. "Yeah, I just…I needed some moral support."

"For what?" I ask.

"I'm going to unfollow Clarke on KamerUhh."

"Oh," I say, smiling encouragingly, but shocked inside that he hasn't already done that. "Good for you."

"I mean I never used to really use my KamerUhh account before he friended me. Like, sometimes, photos of pretty things I saw, maybe, but..." He nods his head firmly. "It's too much. Him and his boyfriend. They do all these sexy posts, and..." He takes a deep breath. "I can do better, right?"

"You absolutely can," I tell him. "Clarke is a jackass. And you liked Andre, right?"

"Yeah!" Harrison smiles. "And...he's only here for a little while, but...there are other options. I really believe that now. Because of you. Someone really great is out there for me, and I'm going to find him, so I should stop lusting after Clarke, and that starts by unfollowing him. Right?"

"Right," I say firmly.

"Okay..." He takes another deep breath and the camera falls a bit so I'm looking up at him at a less flattering angle. In his eyes I can see the reflection of the screen, not clearly, but the colors change as he enters the KamerUhh app, and then his finger rises up and comes down with all the grandeur and finality of the end of a Bach symphony.

There's a long pause, and I watch his expression—it

wavers, like he might refollow at any moment, but then he sucks in his lower lip and closes the app.

"Done," he says.

"Very good work," I say to him.

"Thank you, Emmett. I couldn't do any of this without you."

"I'll see you tomorrow at Georgia's party for John," I say, though I've been considering skipping it. But clearly Harrison will still need me to be there, to make sure things go well with Andre, to give him the encouragement he needs.

"Can I call you tomorrow, so you can look at my outfits?"

"Of course," I say. I hear Dad's key in the front door lock. "But I need to go," I say quickly. "Tomorrow!"

"Bye!" he says.

I manage to hang up on him and open up the good pizza app just as Dad comes in.

"Green peppers okay?" I ask him.

"Do I look good in green, though?" Harrison asks. He's on-screen again, but I've had him set his phone on his desk at a nice angle so he can model different outfits for me.

"You look good in most things," I tell him. "Your coloring is lovely. It's the fit I'm worried about. Show off your body a little more. Not too much. Loose is all right—as long as it's tight in some places."

He nods, confused, and fishes out another pair of jeans, stripping and trying them on in front of me. How does he own so many pairs of ill-fitting jeans?

"Maybe something a little tighter than that, though," I say, hoping that will lead us to the good part of his closet. If it exists. We go on for nearly forty minutes before we settle on a simple black V-neck and some pale jeans that either aren't as bad as the others or are just like the others, but I was so desperate for something I made myself see them as better.

When that's done, I turn to my own much more generous sartorial selection and put on a nice pair of pink pants and floral polo shirt, then drive over there, arriving only half an hour late. Georgia said John would show up at nine, and it's eight thirty when I get in, but the party is already in full swing.

Georgia's place is more ranch style—rustic wood on the walls and roof—at the end of a long tree-lined drive, which is currently festooned with towering candy cane decorations, thrust into the landscape at precarious angles like a postapocalyptic production of *The Nutcracker*. Her Hollywood producer father is originally from Oregon or something, so he likes that cabin-in-the-woods feel, and inside is all warm wood with handwoven tapestries and framed movie posters hanging on the walls.

In one corner is a blown-glass Christmas tree, clear, with colorful spheres and lights hanging inside it, and around the rest of the room are lavish hanging plants with long vines that have been wrapped around the room like garlands, grazing the posters and vanishing behind the tapestries, making it feel like the woods outside have broken in through a window.

The place smells like whiskey, sweat, and expensive fir-scented candles. There's a bar cart in one corner with a bunch of freshmen around it, and a bunch of juniors are hanging out on the landing just over the front door, building a pyramid from red Solo cups on the banister for that KamerUhh challenge. Music is playing loudly, and people are dancing, Taylor and West among them, Taylor grinding on West in a way I find a bit undignified, but I'm not one to judge. In a corner, Andre is chatting up Harrison.

I hang back, watching them, and feeling pleased. They're smiling, talking quickly, Andre using his hands a lot. There's chemistry there. I definitely did a good job this time. I mix myself a drink but stay to the side of the room, unnoticed, watching them flirt and feeling something warm inside me. I did this. Look how happy Harrison is. That's because of me.

Well, because of Andre. But I gave him Andre. No, that sounds creepy. I introduced them knowing they'd hit it off. I did that. And now my friend is happy.

"Apparently, they're both really into upcycled textiles," Taylor says, suddenly next to me, watching me watch Harrison and Andre.

"Are they?" I smile, turning to her. "And it seems like there's some chemistry."

"There is," she says, rolling her eyes. "It's a good match."

"Thank you."

"But Andre would be good for you, too."

"Maybe," I concede. "But—"

"You don't want a boyfriend, you do want a boyfriend, you don't want a boyfriend. I get it, you're not ready."

"Actually, I was going to say, I don't want a breakup. But I do want a boyfriend. That's what I've realized." Because I don't want to fall apart like my dad did, like I told Knight. And maybe they were right that that's normal and not something to worry about, but…they don't have my father. I flinch. What an awful thing to think.

She laughs. "That's what we all want, isn't it? A relationship that will never end. That's perfect from the start." She nudges me with her shoulder. "I get it now. A Perfect Relationship for Perfect Emmett."

"Well, I never settle for anything less than that," I say, grinning. "I have a perfect best friend, and a perfect life—why would I bother with an imperfect relationship? Yours is perfect."

She scoffs. "No, it isn't."

"Flowers and leaves literally swirl around you when you kiss, like you're in a movie," I say.

"That was the art exhibit, that's all."

"It's not just at the art exhibit!"

"What are you talking about?" She shakes her head, laughing. "Look, it's not perfect. We have to work on stuff—like when I get anxious about my art, or when he worries about being the only one of his family who will be on another coast and suddenly feels like he has to choose between me and them."

"Does he really feel that way?" I ask. "He's so... steady."

"Sometimes. But we talk it through. We work on it."

"Well, it looks awfully perfect from where I'm standing."

She smiles like she has a secret. "Only because you're outside. You'll see when you have a boyfriend. In fact... I think that's who you should set up next. You've done all this matchmaking. Find someone for you."

"Oh, I don't know, my twenty-five rule still makes a lot of sense, you know. Perfect now might not be perfect when my brain is fully developed and—"

"Oh my god, no, not that again. Come dance with me." She starts dancing, moving farther into the crowd, and I follow her, taking her hand and dropping my drink and dancing for a moment, losing myself in the music. It's not the best music, not the string quartets at school I find so soothing, but it's fun, with strong drums and bass, and it makes me move in ways that feel like a celebration.

"What's going on there?" Taylor asks, nodding at the door. Miles has just come in, and he looks tired. Maybe he really was sick. But he's making a beeline for Harrison and Andre, waving at them. And Harrison waves back, breaking the flirting he had with Andre, and suddenly it occurs to me: What if the guy Miles meant wasn't straight?

What if it's Harrison?

A guy he's been spending more time with, who he's seen more of, who made him want to suddenly kiss him? That could easily be Harrison. It would explain why he's been so against me setting him up with anyone. Why he hated the idea of Harrison with Clarke. Why he was so repulsed by my offer, and hasn't been speaking to me... because I've slept with the one guy he has feelings for. And I've just paired that guy with a charming and flirty college boy...and...

I watch Miles hug Harrison and shake Andre's hand.

No. I don't like this. It's like riding a horse at full gallop that's suddenly stopped, flinging me off.

What I like is Harrison and Andre together. And this is going to ruin that. I can't let that happen. And besides, they would never work out anyway: Miles might think he likes Harrison, but no one is ever good enough for Miles. Harrison certainly isn't. He's wonderful, but he's just not good enough for Miles. No one could ever be. And Miles must know that.

"He's going to ruin this," I tell Taylor. "Let's go get him out of there so they can keep flirting."

Taylor laughs. "Oh no, I told you whose matchmaker I want to play. This is all you."

I sigh. "Fine," I say, leaving the dance floor and going over to where the three of them are.

"Emmett!" Andre says, spotting me first with a big smile. "I didn't see you come in."

"Just a few minutes ago," I say. "Taylor wanted a dance. Some party, huh?"

"Yeah," Andre says. "West said it was for some friend who's been away?"

"He'll be here soon," Harrison says. "Do we need to hide and yell 'Surprise!' or something?"

"I think he knows about the party," I say.

Miles is quiet and not meeting my eyes again. Rude.

"Hi, Miles," I say sweetly.

"Emmett," he says, his voice cautious.

"I actually need your help with something for Taylor," I say. "Help me out?"

There's a pause long enough that we can all tell he wants to say no. "Sure," he says.

"We'll be back in a sec," I say, leading him away, to the kitchen, which is emptier, and quieter. It's all wood here, too, but with dark green tile, and a big window that looks out on a small pond and some trees, lit by a few lanterns.

"What is it?" Miles asks.

"Why have you been avoiding me?" I ask. "Not even texting back?" I swallow, waiting for him to tell me about his feelings for Harrison.

He looks down and scratches the back of his neck. "Look…Emmett…" He sighs. I can feel my pulse in my wrists, pounding like the plucked strings of violins. Why does it bother me so much—Miles and Harrison? I mean, I don't think it would work, but that shouldn't *bother* me. Maybe it's just that it'll show what a poor matchmaker I am. A failure. Can't see the things right in front of me.

"I just thought we could use a little time apart," he says finally.

I raise an eyebrow and feel myself crossing my arms, defensive. Angry.

"Apart?" I ask. My voice doesn't sound nice. Why wouldn't he just tell me about his feelings for Harrison? Tell me I'm a failure in his condescending Miles way?

"After what you…offered," he says. "I wanted a little time apart."

I can't tell if this is just an excuse, but I roll my eyes anyway, because if it is, it's a terrible one.

"I didn't profess my undying love for you, Miles. I offered you some sex. It's not a big deal."

"It is to me."

"I know, because you don't do casual sex, and I'm sorry, and I said I'm sorry. What do I need to do to show you that?" The words spill out of me sounding exasperated, but they're nicer than what I was going to say, which is that he's being a coward and he should just call me a failure and declare his adoration for Harrison. Just say it. I don't know why I don't tell him to.

"No," he says. "You did. It's me. I just feel like maybe—"

Suddenly, the kitchen door slams open, Georgia grinning maniacally. "He just pulled in!" she squeals. "Come out to say hi."

Miles heads right out the door before Georgia can get out of the way, that's how eager he is to leave. Well, fine, he doesn't want to tell me how I've messed up. For once. I'm sure he's just thinking of how to say it in the most condescending way he can.

"You okay?" Georgia asks as I follow her out of the kitchen.

"Fine," I say. "Let's welcome John back."

She squeezes my shoulder, excited. "I'm so happy he's back, Emmett. You have no idea."

"I think I have some idea," I say with a laugh.

Out in the main room, everyone is staring at the front door, except the juniors still stacking Solo cups on the banister. Georgia lowers the music. The front door opens, and John walks in. He looks good, I'll give him that. Raven hair, bright smile, and I think his jaw got a little stronger while he was away. He's wearing a shirt he clearly got in Paris, though—the cut is trim and short.

He'll probably pepper his English with overenunciated French now; he's that type.

He looks around the room, beaming, and then he stops, his face going blank with shock—and then joy. A full intense joy, the kind you hardly ever see on people's faces in real life. Joy the way Taylor and West look at each other. I look to see who he's looking at.

It's Andre, whose expression matches John's.

Suddenly, almost in slow motion, Andre is running for John. And then they're kissing, embracing, really, and one of the juniors knocks their tower over, sending a flurry of red Solo cups raining down around the pair of them like flower petals. They don't even seem to notice. Andre takes John's face in his hands and kisses it again.

"I *knew* you met someone in Paris!" Georgia shouts.

John and Andre break, still looking at each other, still beaming, then laughing.

"Yes," John says. "We met in Paris. Two Americans studying abroad, but we knew we were only there for a while, so we agreed not to tell each other about home, and instead just spent time together. And we...I never thought I'd see you again. I deleted your number; I was afraid I'd see it, and it would just hurt...but how?"

"It's destiny," Andre says, somehow without a trace of irony.

They kiss again, the red Solo cups like roses blooming at their feet, and Georgia squeals and starts to clap, and then for some reason everyone starts clapping as John and Andre kiss, and kiss again, and then the music gets turned up, and they start to dance. Andre is even crying. Ridiculous, really.

But also, I realize, I wish someone would kiss me like that. I wish red Solo cups would rain down on me. Or flower petals. Or snow. And someone would put their hands around my waist and pull me close. . . . I shake my head. And then I realize—this is another failure. Andre has John, which means he's not interested in Harrison anymore.

Damn.

I'm really not very good at this after all. So much for perfection. So much for Emmett who's good at everything and can find people love and can make sure that a nice boy like Harrison finds someone great, even if it's just so he doesn't fall for . . . me. Maybe it was my intentions. Maybe it's me, and because of my mother, my father, I'm so afraid of what real love might look like. . . .

I shake my head. Now is not the time to feel sorry for myself. Because someone else is probably feeling much worse, and it's all my fault. Again. I look around for Harrison, to make sure he's all right, and I spot him, smiling as Miles hands him a drink.

I walk over.

"Sorry," I say, and my voice isn't as bright as I try to make it. "I let you down, again."

"What?" Harrison asks. "Emmett, there's no way you possibly could have known something as wild as everything John just said."

"You're not psychic," Miles adds.

"I know," I say, because I can tell he meant *perfect* instead of *psychic*. Good to see he's going back to being regular Miles.

"Emmett," Harrison says, "really, don't worry about it." He glances sidelong at Miles like a knife glint. "I've been thinking maybe...I'll be all right."

"I just want you to be happy," I say, though the words taste spoiled.

"I'm disappointed, sure," Harrison says with a shrug. "He was fun to flirt with. But I'm fine. I'm happy. I promise."

"What a romantic story, right?" says a voice next to me. It's Robert, from the environmental club. Has he been here the whole time? "Away in Paris, meeting a guy you know it can't last with, making a deal to just live in the moment. There was this piece in Vox that was kind of like that. This woman went to Spain—"

"The Riddle Hunter story!" Harrison says. "That was way more random than this, though. They kept bumping into each other. The rainstorm in Barcelona?"

"It really was destiny," Robert says.

"What story is this?" Miles asks, grinning.

"Oh, you have to read it," Harrison says. "It's from like three weeks ago, I think?"

"I have it," Robert says, already on his phone. "Emailing it to you. You too, Emmett."

"Thanks," I say, and sigh. I look at Miles, smiling like an idiot at Harrison. There's one match left, and it's so obvious, but I'm loath to make it. I don't know why. I just feel like Miles is…he's my oldest friend. Even before Taylor. And I might hate him sometimes, but I never really saw him with anyone before. I never pictured his future wife, even when I thought he was straight. When I pictured his future, he was always with…me. Just there. Like he always has been. But that was selfish, I know. Unkind. To make him into an accessory in my future. My oldest friend, applauding when I cured cancer, hugging me when I accepted an award, telling me he believed in me. Us visiting those ruins in Scotland he loves so much, him thrilled to be with such old things, me making jokes about it to friends after. He doesn't owe me any of that. And it's not like I ever expressed any of this to him. We go days without speaking. If it weren't for our parents and proximity, I'm sure we would have faded from each other's lives years ago. And the thought of that hurts me, like a syringe in my gut. Because now he *is* gone. When a finger is cut off completely, it doesn't leave a scar with a nice story.

He'd hate me rolling my eyes at the ruins, though, and he'd be so annoyed at my ego when I help cure cancer. This is better. Him and Harrison. I still think Harrison isn't good enough, but Miles does. That's what matters. Right?

"Hey, come get a drink with me, Robert?" I say. They should be left alone to fall in love. So something can fall on them—maybe the ceiling will start shedding paint flecks. They'll look like snow.

"Huh?" Robert asks.

"I like the color of what you're drinking. I want you to make me one."

"Oh!" He smiles, happy. "Yeah, cool. Here, come with me. It's mostly orange juice, but…" I follow him to the bar cart, glancing back once at Miles and Harrison. Harrison is going on about the article, but Miles is looking at me, confused. I smile back at him, though it feels sad. I'm giving him what he wants, right?

"So, you take some grenadine, right, and you stir that in first. Then a splash of vodka, but more importantly, some tequila. I used to think you wanted a drink to be super strong so you can get drunk faster, but I think I've come to appreciate the flavor now, too."

"You used to think that?" I ask, laughing. "Harrison bought that at a party recently."

"Oh no," Robert says with a laugh. "Did he get very drunk?"

"Yes," I say.

Robert looks over my shoulder at them. "I bet it was cute, though. He's so smart about so many things—his ideas for water purification systems are going to change the world, if he can get the funding. But of course he's a doof about alcohol."

"Doof?" I say. "Wait, water purification?"

"Oh yeah. We talk about it all the time. He's just... great."

I sigh. He really loves Harrison. And they really would have been good together. NPR. Environmental causes. And Robert isn't bad-looking. Just because I thought he wasn't good enough for Harrison...but Harrison clearly thought he was. And then I got in the way. Maybe I'm not as nice as I think I am. Maybe sometimes, I'm actually pretty terrible when I'm trying to be nice.

"Anyway," Robert says, handing me the drink, "what do you think?"

I swirl it and take a long drink. It's nice, actually. Bright and salty.

"It's very good," I say.

"It's pretty strong, too," Robert says. "Maybe slow down."

"I'll be fine," I say. "And I deserve it. I'm realizing today that maybe I've screwed a lot of things up lately."

"You?" Robert laughs. "I doubt that. You're so nice."

I laugh. "Not today. Not... ever, maybe."

"Well," Robert says. "None of us are perfect. All we

can do is try, right? Oscar Wilde said if you shoot for the moon, you'll still land among the stars."

I smile. It's a nice thought, landing among the stars. But not tonight.

"I'm going to go dance, I think," I tell Robert. "Thank you for the drink. And talking. You're a good guy."

"Awww, thanks, Emmett. You too." We toast with our glasses, and then I walk to the dance floor, where everyone is still dancing up a storm, thrilled by the love story of John and Andre—who have conspicuously vanished. I find Taylor dancing with West and Georgia, the three of them laughing and talking about John and Andre's kiss.

"I swear I really had no idea," West says. "Andre never said a thing."

"Still very suspicious," Taylor says, laughing.

"I'm just so happy for them," Georgia says. "Such a great love."

"Yeah," I say.

"Oh, what's wrong with you?" Taylor says. Then she nods. "Ah, you think of this as another failure. Well, not even you can be good at everything. I like this for you. Perfect except for one meaningless skill."

"It's not meaningless," I say. "It was about making people happy."

"What?" Georgia asks. "Emmett, don't be so sad. We'll find someone for you, too."

I laugh. "I'm not worried about me."

Georgia lays her hands on my wrist, pitying. "Don't worry. We all know you had a crush on John, Emmett. But you're going to meet a guy—"

I pull my wrist away and turn on Georgia, failing to repress the sneer on my lip. "I did not have a crush on John, Georgia. I barely knew him, just like I barely knew you until you insisted on sitting with us this semester and I was too nice to tell you to go away. Just because John is your entire personality doesn't mean he's everyone else's."

Oh. I didn't mean to say all that. This drink is stronger than I thought.

Georgia looks like I punched her. Even Taylor and West are staring at me like I've just done something vile. I look around. A lot of people are looking at me. Harrison. Miles. His eyes are so disappointed.

I laugh. "And that's what you get for assuming I have a crush," I say, my voice light. It was a joke, I'm trying to say to everyone. Just a joke.

Georgia, thankfully, smiles, even though her eyes are watery. She forces a laugh.

"Sorry," she says. "You're right. I shouldn't joke about that." She laughs again. And I laugh, too, and people turn away. But I can still feel Miles's eyes on me. Taylor's, too. She takes my wrist.

"I gotta pee," Georgia says, taking off. She was definitely crying. I did something very...not nice.

"Emmett…," Taylor says softly.

"I should go," I say. And I turn and walk away.

Outside, the music is softer, and I sit down behind one of the candy canes, hiding from people coming in and out, until I'm sober enough to drive home. Taylor texts me, but I ignore it.

Today was a failure in so many ways, I realize as I get home. Today I was a failure. And it's not a disease or because of my mother dying, or anything like that.

It's just me. It's who I am. A failure—at matchmaking, at understanding love, and at being the one thing I always thought I was: nice.

chapter eleven

WHEN I WAKE UP SUNDAY, I HAVE A LOT OF TEXTS FROM TAYLOR, asking how I am. Not from anyone else, though. Which is fair. What I deserve. I should fix this, I think. Make sure Harrison finds love, make Miles my friend again, and...apologize to Georgia. But I don't know how. What do I say? What do I do?

Downstairs, Dad has put presents under the tree and unlit candles in the menorah. It's Christmas Eve and the first night of Hanukkah tonight.

"Jas, Pri, and Miles are all coming over tonight," Dad says. He's making some kind of smoothie with the green tea. It's very brightly colored. "We're all going to make those latkes together, but Jas said it'll be you and me leading—she'll just make sure we do it right. Won't that be nice?"

"It'll be great," I say, sitting down. I do not want to face Miles today. He's going to be condescending and for once I'll deserve it. I hate that. And maybe he and Harrison hooked up last night, and he'll tell me about it, and thinking about that makes my stomach whir like the green smoothie in the blender.

"I'm not hungry," I say when Dad puts it down in front of me. "If anything, I'm nauseous."

Dad reaches out and lays his hand on my forehead. "No fever," he says. "But we can take some bl—" He stops himself. "We can make an appointment with the doctor."

I smile and raise an eyebrow. "The doctor?"

"Yes..." Dad sips his own smoothie. "Last night, while you were at the party, Jas and Pri had me over for drinks and they said they were...worried. About you. About me. Me, mostly. They thought maybe I had some anxiety about your mother's death, which I was taking out on you. Apparently drawing blood when you don't want it drawn is...abuse. Which I'd never thought about before but soon as they said it, Emmett...I..." He stretches out his hands and takes mine. "I'm so sorry. That wasn't right."

"Dad, I never let you take it unless I was all right with it."

"Still," he says. "I guess I've been...anyway. Priyanka knows a psychologist who specializes in this kind of thing. So I have an appointment with him."

I smile. "Really?"

"Your mother used to say something—something Priyanka reminded me of last night. She used to say that people were always growing, our brains always taking in new information. And we could either take it in and grow, make ourselves better. Or we could reject it, and close our minds off. I've been closing my mind off. All I see is you dying like your mom and it's made me so afraid that..." He takes a long, slow breath. "Anyway. She'd be pretty annoyed with me. That's what Pri said, and she was... right. I'm so ashamed, Emmett." He squeezes my hand.

"Dad, it's okay. Really. I love you. And I think Mom would be pretty annoyed with both of us."

"Oh? Have you also been obsessing over your son's health?"

I laugh. "No. I mean...I don't know. I think I've just been trying to prove how nice I am to the world, and I have been failing, and last night I...said something unkind to someone."

"Unkind?"

"Kind of cruel."

"Emmett..." He looks sad. "Why did you say it?"

"I was feeling like I'd screwed things up. And...I don't know. I was angry at myself." And I felt like I'd lost Miles, I realize. Like he was going to live a happy life with Harrison and I'd never see him again. And maybe that's what he always wanted. I think it's what I wanted, too, until I saw it happening in front of me.

"And I was afraid of…losing someone, I think? Like, someone I didn't even know I cared that much about, but now he's probably never going to talk to me again, and… the girl I was cruel to, she thought I was upset about something else. And she said something…not accurate. And sort of rude. But not cruel. Not the way I was. But I unleashed a lot on her. And now I think everyone is mad at me. And they should be."

Dad nods. "You were afraid of losing someone so you went a little nuts, huh?" He smiles. "Maybe you should make an appointment with this shrink, too."

"Maybe," I say. "But I don't think we're supposed to see the same psychologist."

"Well, then he can recommend someone. If you want."

"It couldn't hurt," I say. "I hate what I said yesterday. I want to…like Mom said. I want to be better."

"Well, your brain is always growing," Dad says. "That's what she used to say. Your brain is always growing."

"Not after twenty-five," I say.

"Oh, she didn't mean it scientifically. She just meant, you always have the choice to be better. To learn. To change."

"Oh," I say, feeling like maybe I've been wrong about a lot of things, for a very long time. It feels like my body is heavy.

"You want some smoothie now?" Dad asks. "It's not bad, I promise."

He nudges a glass over to me and I take a sip. He's right. It's not bad. It's not especially good. But it's not bad.

"And when you're done with that, go wrap your gifts for everyone and put them under the tree. Jasmine gave me a grocery list, so we need to hit the store later."

"Okay," I say, smiling.

Upstairs I take out the gifts I have for everyone. For Dad I bought a whole new gardening set—pruners, gloves, straw hat, all in a shade that's the color of green tea. For Jasmine, I found some new spatulas with little owls painted on them. And for Priyanka, I do the same thing every year—ballet flats. Comfortable ones. Doctors go through them like tissues. But I was especially proud of what I'd done for Miles. From a photo, I painted a ruined castle in Scotland, in the snow, very romantic, and then I found a place that printed it on a fleece blanket, just like the one he steals every time he comes over. I think about not giving it to him, but that would be petty at this point, and besides, it's a fitting end. The blanket was the only thing he'll miss in the house, so now he doesn't have to. Well, and my dad, maybe. I take it out to fold it up, but it looks cheaper than I remembered. Like maybe I've never really known what Miles wanted. What anyone wanted. Still... I'll give it to him. On the shelf the stuffed rabbit and Helena agree. Miles is going to be happy with Harrison, and that's all I want, right?

I wrap the gifts and bring them downstairs to go

under the tree, and after I shower, Dad and I go to the store, where they are dangerously low on potatoes, but we scavenge enough for the latkes as Dad wiggles to the piped-in Christmas music.

As we drive home and I realize Miles and his moms will be over soon, I think about trying to get out of it. I think about Miles, probably smiling and happy. I wonder if he and Harrison kissed last night. I wonder if they did more. I know Harrison's body enough that I can picture it, can see Miles making him moan, and it makes me feel carsick. If I tell Dad I'm not feeling well, I'll bet he'll cancel. I'll beg him to take my blood, say I have to go to the hospital...except he just had a breakthrough. And I would undo all that.

I swallow. I can deal with it. Miles is happy. It shouldn't bother me, him and Harrison being together. Harrison gets a boyfriend, like I always wanted. Maybe it's just that it's one I didn't pick out for him. That's why I feel sick. Just ego. I should be able to swallow that down. At least for tonight. For the holidays.

We spend the rest of the day cleaning and decorating, putting the star on the tree—a beautiful blue glass one that has ropes of thin blue lights that pour down from it and wind around the rest of the tree. We make and hang extravagant garden-grown pink-and-white garlands in the foyer, put candles up. I artfully arrange some spare Christmas baubles and a dreidel on the entry table. Flowers are everywhere. I'll make the house feel as merry as I don't. Maybe that'll cheer me up. And after tonight, I'll hide myself away for a while, and reemerge when school starts, and people will remember me as the butterfly I am, not the bully who can't even find a boyfriend for the friend he's sleeping with.

I turn that last phrase over in my mind, wondering if it sounds ridiculous.

No. It's accurate.

When Miles and his moms show up, I'm dressed in my holiday best: a glittery blue-and-green sweater and red pants. Dad has a hideous Christmas sweater complete with a three-dimensional Santa beard. But Jasmine and Priyanka are not to be outdone, in matching Christmas pajamas, and Miles, clearly unhappy about it, has on a coordinating sweater. Though it is tamer than Dad's. Slightly.

"I brought extra candles because I was away for Diwali," Priyanka says, her arms filled. "The weatherman said it might snow tonight!"

"Really?" I ask.

"Four percent chance," Miles says. I sigh.

Jasmine and Miles are carrying platters of food and the moment they enter, the house feels so much warmer and alive. It smells like cinnamon and fruit, and Priyanka starts lighting candles and putting them everywhere, so the smell of warm wax mingles. With just a kiss on the cheek for both me and Dad, Jasmine heads to the kitchen, and the smell of warm oil joins the olfactory symphony. It smells like a home. I look over at Miles as he puts some gifts under the tree. I thought he'd be glowing, finally with Harrison, but maybe neither of them had the nerve to proclaim their feelings last night. If I still thought I was any good at this matchmaking I'd probably urge them to do something about that. But not with Miles.

And he won't look at me. That's probably about Georgia. I wouldn't look at me, either.

I sit on the sofa and sigh, not sure what to do. This is going to be a lonely holiday.

Miles starts hunting for the fleece blanket. I throw it at him, and he catches it with a smile, then sits down next to me.

"So...last night," he says.

I raise an eyebrow. I thought he wanted distance.

"I know," he says. "Look, maybe I phrased it wrong. You're, like, my closest friend, Emmett. I just...didn't want you to keep apologizing. I just need to...figure stuff out. But I'm still your friend. And you...are clearly upset."

I smile a little. Relieved, slightly, that we're done fighting, or whatever we were. That I'm forgiven for at least one mistake.

"A little better now."

He smiles, but it's a little sad. I know what he's thinking. It's what I'm thinking, too.

"But I was pretty awful," I say. "To Georgia. I know. You don't have to tell me."

He shrugs. "I mean, Taylor told me what she'd said, about you having a crush on John, and that wasn't great, either, but you...responded harshly."

"I wasn't nice."

"No."

"I'm supposed to be nice."

He laughs. "Emmett, it's okay not to be nice."

"I try to be, though."

"Well...then go apologize."

"What?" I say. "Like...physically go to her house?"

"Yeah."

"What would I even say? Sorry, I was angry that all my matchmaking attempts had failed and I took it out on you?"

"Is that all it was?"

"I mean...I've always found her kind of annoying."

"I've always found *you* kind of annoying, doesn't mean we're not friends."

I glare at him, and he laughs. It feels normal, for a moment, like it did last time he was here, just a few weeks ago, before I decided to become a matchmaker and discovered I was terrible at it.

"I just don't know if I...she wouldn't even want to see me."

"Come on." He stands up, casting off the blanket, and offers me his hand. "I'll go with you."

"Really?" I ask. "Because you like watching me admit I'm wrong?"

"Because I believe you're better than what you said last night. I don't care if you're nice, Emmett. I never have. I care that you're a good person. And a good person apologizes when they're in the wrong. So come on."

He reaches down and pulls me up.

"You'll even let her see you in that sweater?" I ask.

"That's how much our friendship means to me," he says.

I smile. "It means a lot to me, too," I say softly. I open my mouth to say more, to say I'm happy for him and Harrison, but the words stick, and instead, I turn to the kitchen, where Jasmine is showing Dad how to squeeze the shredded potato.

"This can't be good for your skin," he says.

"It's worth it for your belly, though," she says, and they laugh together.

"We have to run out for a moment. We'll be back soon," I say.

"Be back by sundown to light the candles," Dad says, eyes focused on the water being squeezed from the potatoes.

"I'll drive," Miles says, and we get into his car.

"What do I even say?" I ask.

"You just say you're sorry," he says. "The rest will come naturally."

"Really? I'm not sure I've ever apologized for anything."

"You apologized to me last week."

"That was different."

"Why?" he asks, his voice suspicious.

"I don't know. You always act like I should be apologizing to you, so it felt like giving you what you wanted."

He laughs. "Well...this is me acting like you should apologize to Georgia, if that helps."

I nod. "It does, actually." And it does. Miles might be condescending, acting like he always knows best, but... he sometimes does. He's someone who, I think, maybe doesn't see me as perfect because he always sees me as being able to do better. I wonder if that's how my mom saw the world, too: People's brains are always growing. They can always do better. Be better. Perfect isn't something you can be. And nice is...just pretending. Nice is nothing. Good is what's important. Being good. And we can always be better at that.

"You okay?" Miles asks. I realize we've been parked in the candy-cane driveway for a few seconds. I nod and get out, and go ring the bell. The sun is already low on the horizon—I don't have much time, which I think is a relief.

Miles hangs back, leaning against his car. I can feel him watching, but instead of it being condescending, like a test, I realize that what it is, is supportive. Yes, he's expecting the best from me—but he also believes in the best from me.

Georgia opens the door. She's in a green silk romper, like a holiday flight suit. She looks confused, then looks behind me and spots Miles and laughs.

"Great sweater," she calls.

"Thanks!" he shouts back.

"Georgia," I say, softer than I mean to. Her eyes flash back to me. She looks...scared. For some reason that's worse than her looking angry.

"It's Christmas Eve," she says.

"I know," I say. "I'll be quick. I wanted to apologize. I'm sorry for what I said yesterday. It was cruel. I was feeling annoyed with myself about a bunch of other things, and I took it out on you, and I shouldn't have. You're a good friend to John, and I shouldn't have made fun of that."

She tilts her head, and her expression softens. "Awww, Emmett...look, I was rude, too. That crack about you having a crush on John wasn't cool. I was just...I don't know. In that moment, I felt like he'd gone away again? Like he was going to go live in Paris and I'd never see him again." She shakes her head. "It's so stupid. I started sitting with you because I thought it was, like, the same, right? Like John was in Paris and Taylor had a new boyfriend and here we were, lonely. Why couldn't we be new best friends?"

"What?" I ask.

"Stupid, I know."

"No...," I say. "Kind of sweet, actually. Though I wish you'd told me that was the plan."

She laughs. "Ugh, no, I would have sounded so pathetic. Let's be friends because our friends are busy. No. So I just did what I always do, which is act like we were already friends. Except I could feel you being like 'What is this girl doing here?' so I kept trying to show you how cool I was—mainly by talking about John. It was awful. I could feel it every day, at the table, just John coming out of my mouth over and over, which just made me miss him more.... I've been a lot. I don't blame you for saying what you said. The fact that you went all semester and let me sit at your table...that was really nice."

"No," I say. "Nice would have actually been making you feel welcome instead of making you feel like the most interesting thing about you was John."

She leans against the doorframe. "Actually, one thing all this taught me—John being away, you, John and Andre's kiss last night with the cups falling everywhere..."

"Ridiculous, right? Like a living romance novel."

"Completely absurd," she agrees, without hesitation. "Almost as bad as Taylor and West. Maybe it's a family thing."

I laugh. "Maybe."

"Anyway, it made me realize that you were kind of

right. I need to live my own life. So this morning, for a Christmas present, I asked my parents if I could take a gap year. No matter where I get in. And I can, like...go to Europe, and travel, and meet hot people, and just... experience stuff. For myself. I realized I've never wanted to do something so badly. They said yes. Is that too wild?"

"No." I shake my head. "I think it's genius. I think you'll have so much fun. And probably bring home some hot significant other to show off."

"Nah." She shakes her head quickly. "I'm with you. No serious romance until your brain is done developing at...twenty-five, right?"

I hear footsteps behind me, Miles getting closer to remind me we have to head home. The sky is dark pink. "Right," I say, then shrug. "But I don't think that's right anymore, actually."

"No?" She looks genuinely surprised. "You've been saying that as long as I've known you."

"Yeah." I look down at my feet. "Apparently my mom... she used to say that the brain was never done growing. I mean, biologically, sure, it's developed at twenty-five, but we can always grow. And so it doesn't matter when you meet someone—what matters is that you can grow together. Like flowers that are planted next to each other, and they wrap around each other as they grow."

Georgia laughs. "Emmett? A romantic?"

"What?" I say.

"That's the most romantic thing I've ever heard from anyone, Emmett. I'm just shocked it came from you." She smiles. "Happy shocked, though. Well, happy for you. I still want to slut it up around Europe."

I laugh. "Then I want that for you."

"And I'm going to send you so many photos," she says. "Because you're my friend...right?"

"Absolutely," I say, and I mean it. She reaches forward and she hugs me, and I hug her back and think about these months of missed opportunities, how we could have really been friends, if only I'd been open to it. Open to growing.

"Sorry, Georgia," Miles says. "We promised our folks we'd be back by sunset."

"Yeah, my parents will want to eat soon, too," she says. "I'm glad you came by, though. Thanks."

"Thank you," I say. "Merry Christmas."

"You too!" she says, going back into her house. "And happy Hanukkah."

She closes the door and I walk back to the car with Miles, wiping my eyes. I'm not crying, of course, that would be silly. It's just that the candy canes are glaring.

"You mean all that, that you said?" Miles asks, starting the car. "About growing together?"

"Oh no, did you hear that?" I feel myself blushing. "All right, make as much fun as you want. I deserve it."

He laughs. "Did you mean it, though?"

"Yes."

He nods and keeps driving in silence. "So you want a boyfriend now?"

"I don't know," I say. That's a lie. "Yes. But they have to be right. They have to be someone who...I can feel their loss when I'm not around them. So that even if it all turns out terrible, even if we break up, it was worth it, because not having been with them would have been worse."

"That sounds like perfection to me," Miles says, and I immediately think of him and who he must mean—Harrison.

"I should apologize to Harrison, too," I say.

"Harrison?" Miles asks.

"Yes, all my misguided matchmaking...I think I made it so much more complicated and painful for him than it needed to be."

Miles chuckles, low. "I don't think you need to worry about that."

"Ah," I say. So they did hook up. Good for them. I wish I felt happier, but instead, I just feel like stone. Maybe this is how Georgia felt seeing John and Andre kiss.

"Ah?" Miles asks.

"I'm happy for him. And congratulations."

"Thank you," Miles says, and my body feels even heavier. "I thought you'd be angry."

"Angry?" I say. "You think that little of me?"

"Well, no," Miles says quickly. "But you have your plans and then I swept in and…"

"He's happy. You're happy. You'll be a cute couple."

Miles slams on the brakes in front of my house. "What?" he asks, almost yells.

I get out of the car, suddenly craving fresh air.

"Emmett," he calls as I walk to the house. "I did not hook up with Harrison."

I turn around. "It's all right. I know he's the one you were talking about. The one you suddenly felt something for."

He laughs, shaking his head as he comes around the car. "I do not believe you."

"Well, then what did you mean I don't need to worry about it, and you swept in?"

"I set him up. Well, barely. I just told him to ask Robert out. That's what I was trying to do last night at the party, but then you dragged Robert away."

"So you two could be together!" I realize I'm shouting, and my hands are flying upward, and I bring them back down. "But…you thought I'd be mad you successfully matched him?"

"Maybe?" Miles laughs. "Sorry. You thought I had a crush on Harrison?"

"Yes. And I was going to set him up with Robert next, but when I saw you were interested, I thought… well…he couldn't do better than you. No one could."

He smiles so large it might light the sky again. "Why did you think I had a crush on Harrison?"

"You were always there to defend him, make him feel better—after I messed up with Clarke, and then with Andre."

"So were you."

"Well, yes, I suppose...I was being a friend."

"So was I." He smiles.

"So it wasn't Harrison?" I ask. A deep relief sweeps through my body and my legs shake, though I'm not sure why.

"You really have no idea, do you?"

"What?"

"Who my crush is on."

I shake my head. "Some straight guy? Someone you haven't told?"

"Well, yeah, but—"

"You didn't want to tell me, which I understand, it's your business, but I don't know why you'd think I'd know."

"Because—"

"Unless you're asking me to make it happen now, which I cannot see, because as we are now very sure of, I am no good at this, Miles. I am staying out of the love game and—"

"It's you, Emmett."

For a moment, the world is silent. All I can hear is his breath, and all I can see is his face, which moves from teasing, his smile shaking, to surprised and then suddenly terrified. The confession burst out of him against his will; he was just trying to mock me, but he did it with the truth, I realize. And then I realize another truth.

I lean forward and kiss him.

He wraps his arms around me, pulling me closer, and I put my arms around his neck as our mouths open, his breath warm on my lips. And then he stops and pulls away.

"Wait," he says.

"I'm sorry," I say.

"No...no. Don't apologize. I wanted that. I want... you, Emmett. You were biting into a peach one day at lunch, and you were saying nice things to Georgia even though it killed you, and making fun of me, and then the next second Taylor said something about her work, and doubting herself, and you, like, snapped to attention, immediately making her feel better about herself, and all I wanted to do in that moment—since that moment—is kiss you. You're infuriating, and I don't think you like me very much sometimes, but when you care about people— Taylor, Harrison, even Georgia—you really care about them. So of course it was you who I first wanted to kiss. I want you. I think some part of me has always wanted you. But...I want you as a boyfriend. I want to, like you said, try growing together. I don't want to be just a—"

I grab his hand, and I weave my fingers through it. "I

do like you. I like you very much. I think that's why I was so rude to Georgia, because I saw you and Harrison and thought... I've liked you, Miles. I had a crush on you for most of ninth grade.... Sorry if I... don't always show it." I put my other hand on his neck, spreading my hand up to stroke his jaw. I haven't always been great to him. But maybe it's because I never quite understood. He always sees the best in me, just like I always see the best for people... even if I might have the wrong idea of what that is. "I want it, too. We'll grow together," I promise him.

He leans forward and kisses me again, and impossibly, it starts to snow, thick flurries of it falling down around us.

I'm blessed, but I'm not perfect. And I'm definitely not always nice. But I try to be good. That's what I tell Harrison by way of an apology. But I'm glad he and Robert are going out now. They had a Hanukkah date and exchanged presents—they had each already gotten something for the other, both from the NPR store. They deserve each other, and I don't think Harrison can do better, because Robert is the best for him. They send me a photo of them in the park, doing volunteer litter cleanup. Leaves are spiraling around them as they laugh, caught in a huge wind.

Taylor and West spend the holiday together, and

with Andre and John. Taylor says John's okay to hang out with, though I would have made a much better brother-in-law. Georgia is already planning her year abroad—Berlin first, then London, then Paris, and finally Barcelona, three months in each. She asked me to go over her resume so she can apply to work at queer community centers as she travels. Clarke and HottestMonth have been getting loads of likes on their couple's content. They've even got a sponsorship: Discernment, a couples counseling app. Watching their sponsored videos makes me laugh so hard green tea comes out of my nose.

As for me and Miles...well, I would have wanted to keep it from our parents for a while, but unfortunately they were watching us from the window for our first kiss, something we found out when we stopped and realized that it wasn't just snowing, but that Priyanka and Jasmine were outside, applauding. That was my immediate worry—that now it's extra messy, because if we break up, it'll be like losing family. But Miles just pointed out what I'd told him—all queer relationships can be messy because all queer people are a kind of family—Family, according to his moms. You just have to agree to remember to love each other, even if you don't end up together. So that was our first promise—even if we don't keep growing together as a couple, even if we break up in one day or twenty years, we still stay in each other's lives. That way we never have to lose each other.

The next promise was to my dad, who was very worried that I was kissing someone, even if he did admit I couldn't have chosen better than Miles. But still…

"Sex, Emmett. Kissing leads to sex!"

This was as we opened our presents under the tree that night. He pulled me aside to whisper it loudly enough that Priyanka, Jasmine, and, more horrifyingly, Miles could hear it. I blushed so hard it choked me, and I couldn't respond.

"Henry, we can hear you," Pri said, trying on her new shoes. "And Emmett knows to use condoms. You've drilled it into him for years. He has the HPV vaccine. So does Miles. Did you want him to be chaste the rest of his life?"

"Well…," Dad said, looking sheepish. "I worry is all."

"Sure," Priyanka said, walking over. "But maybe those worries aren't to share with Emmett. They're to share with Dr. Leigh."

He took a deep breath. "Yes, all right. Just…" He looked at me, eyes wide. "Use a condom."

"I will, Dad," I said, my mouth finally working again.

Miles came over after that, his new fleece blanket wrapped around him like a cape, and threw it over our heads, so it was a tent for a moment, and kissed me again. I like kissing him.

"Condoms, huh?" he asked. "Moving kind of fast. Making assumptions."

"Well, as you know, I'm excellent at spotting chemistry," I said.

He smirked, and it occurred to me that just a few hours ago, I would have found that smirk condescending, but then I saw it for what it was—teasing. Loving. Finding me endlessly amusing. I kissed him again.

"We didn't mean you should use the condoms right now," Priyanka said loudly, making us both blush this time, and immediately uncover ourselves from the blanket and move to opposite sides of the sofa. Our parents laughed very loudly at that.

And when we started telling people, everyone else was apparently not at all surprised at our newfound coupledom. Taylor even mentioned something about a betting pool, but when I asked what she meant, she said she was joking. I'm not sure if she was. But it all falls very easily into place. Taylor and West, Harrison and Robert, me and Miles. He's still insufferably condescending sometimes, but I know he just thinks I can be better. And I can.

Also he claims that sometimes *I'm* also insufferably condescending.

I don't see it, personally.

I'm still terrified of loss. Sometimes, I think about us breaking up, or about him dying suddenly. I talk to my psychologist about it, and she tells me that it's normal to worry. What's important is not dwelling on those worries. After all, she says, what if we don't break up, what if we live to be a hundred together? Would I give that up just because we might break up?

The answer comes back like the music of a string quartet—no. An entire orchestra: never.

So maybe the relationship isn't perfect. That's all right, nothing is. Maybe we hope it'll be something, and it turns out to be something else, maybe we find areas we have to work on, and maybe our friends joke about us teasing each other. None of that matters. What matters is how happy we are now, growing together. Something I'm constantly reminded of when leaves, flowers, and once a stray bag of shredded paper that wasn't well tied, all seem to fall on us at any moment.

But I don't mind it when he picks the petals out of my hair or off my shoulder. I don't mind it that my outfits are covered in something.

I like it, in fact. I like the mess.

A NOTE OF PROFOUNDEST APPRECIATION

Dearest Reader,

Though you might suppose, owing to my name standing alone on the cover of this novel, that authorship is a solitary profession, you would find, happily for me at least, that that is not so. I owe much gratitude to the many helpers and worthy intellectuals who lent me their aid in creating the vision as found within these pages.

First, I must honor my agent, the Contessa Joy T—— of Massachusetts, who has remained steadfast in my representation for more years than I'd care to reveal here. Though I have been at times troublesome, she has always endured my fits of distemper while cultivating my flights of fancy. Indeed, everyone at the David Black Agency has proven themselves the warmest of friends and most valiant of defenders.

Much credit is due my editor, Lady Alvina L—— of New York, who, upon seeing the earliest version of these pages, took it upon herself to assist me in fixing them with vigor and good humor. Like the most devoted and honest of dressmakers, she pointed out flaws to be resewn and where trim might best flatter my figure, and even when I resisted such commendable improvements, she continued to show them to me in different light and angles until I understood that she was, and always had been, correct, and took it upon myself to make her suggested adjustments. Her assistance was itself assisted by Ms. Ruqayyah D—— and Mr. Ben H——, those eminent helpers who would hold up mirrors to my writing to help me best see the problems—and wonders—of my work.

The art of speaking a book to life might be primarily my domain, but speaking a book into the world is a much more complicated affair. Making sure people are aware that the book exists in the sea of literature that is constantly replenishing itself requires one to be both captain and lighthouse, and I'm so grateful that the Baroness Cheryl L—— of New Jersey has taken on those roles with such faith and steadfastness. In fact, I have many such captains on the ocean of the literate world; Ms. Marisa R——, who oversees many ships, Major Victoria S——, Ms. Christie M——, and Ms. Amber M—— are to be praised especially for their work with children and the proletariat, while Ms. Andie D——, Ms. Savannah K——, Mme. Emilie P——, and Lady Jacqueline E—— have done great works in overseeing the distribution of flyers and the like for the promotion of this work.

Though it is a truth universally acknowledged that one ought not to judge a book by its cover, it is often unavoidable that the cover, being the first thing one sees, has some impact. To ensure that such impact is grand and inspiring, much work is required. In the case of this novel, dear reader, I was blessed by the artistic charms of the artist Ms. Allison R——, who created a true marvel of a cover, as well as the designers, Mr. Patrick H—— and Ms. Sasha I——, for assisting in making sure such art is properly maintained and presented.

In fact, the entire crew at Little, Brown Books for Young Readers have proven themselves time and time again more than capable of rising to the challenge of publishing such novels as my own, which in these trying times is not the ease and delight it once was. I am most grateful to Ms. Marisa F—— and Ms. Patricia A——, who oversaw the production of this particular novel, and Ms. Megan T——, who oversees the entire company with aplomb.

I would be lost without my salons, which are filled with other writers and artists. These fine authors and visionaries never cease to inspire me and ease the burdens of the mind, which come from embarking on such an unwise venture as writing a novel. They are the Duchess Dahlia A——, Captain August C——, Captain Cory M——, Mr. Adam S——, the Marquis Tom R——, Mr. Adib K——, Mr. Charles L——, Sir Julian

W——, Viscount Caleb R——, and Mr. Cale D——. Many thanks to them for refined company and charitable offers of comfort and conversation.

And a special note of thanks to Ms. Maggie R——, Ms. Nicola Y——, and Ms. Sandhya M——, whose presence in our salon on Romance was so inspiring to me to take what was but a seed of an idea at the time and encourage it to blossom.

Family is always important, to guarantee one's upbringing is filled with culture and taste, and while my family could not quite provide the latter with as much spirit as was needed for one of my refinement, they did give it their all, and I am eternally grateful for their love, support, and encouragement.

And as always, I must give my eternal thanks to Mr. Christopher S——, who, by his mere presence, reaffirms and reassures me.